AN **UNOFFICIAL** GAMER'S NOVEL

THE
FOR THE
DIAMOND SWORD

Also by Winter Morgan

The Mystery of the Griefer's Mark

AN **UNOFFICIAL** GAMER'S NOVEL

THE QUEST
FOR THE
DIAMOND SWORD

WINTER MORGAN

SIMON AND SCHUSTER

First published in Great Britain in 2015
by Simon & Schuster UK Ltd
A CBS company
Originally published in the USA in 2014 by Sky Pony Press

10 9 8 7 6 5 4 3

Simon & Schuster UK Ltd
1st Floor, 222 Gray's Inn Road
London WC1X 8HB

A CIP catalogue record for this book
is available from the British Library

The Quest for the Diamond Sword: An Unofficial Gamer's Novel
is an original work of fan fiction that is not associated with
Minecraft or MojangAB. It is not sanctioned nor has it been
approved by the makers of Minecraft.

PB ISBN: 978-1-4711-4392-2
Ebook ISBN: 978-1-4711-4393-9

Printed and bound by CPI Group (UK) Ltd, Croydon, CR0 4YY

www.simonandschuster.co.uk

TABLE OF CONTENTS

LIFE ON THE FARM

Steve wasn't a risk taker. he lived a simple life on a flourishing wheat farm, where he grew carrots, potatoes, and pumpkins and bred pigs. Afternoons were spent talking to Eliot the blacksmith or Avery the librarian, who lived in the nearby village. In the village, he'd trade wheat and coal for emeralds.

He used the emeralds to adorn the walls of his home. Yet that morning, he decided to head to town and exchange some of his extra emeralds for iron. Steve wanted to craft iron armor. Although he never planned on using it, he was cautious and knew it was important to have armor. He also liked crafting things.

Eliot was in his shop when Steve arrived and said, "Hi, Steve. Looking for more emeralds?"

"No," Steve took out the emeralds, "I have too many. I'd like to exchange them for iron ingots."

"What are you going to do with iron?" Eliot asked as he gave Steve the blocks. "Build another Golem? You were so nice to build that for our village."

"Thanks, but I want to craft armor," replied Steve.

"Are you going on an adventure?" Eliot couldn't believe his ears. Steve was the last person he'd expect to want armor or go on an adventure.

"I hope not!" Steve smiled, "I just thought it would be good to have in my inventory."

"Enjoy crafting, Steve." Eliot gave him the iron ignots.

On the way home, Steve ran into Avery the librarian, who said, "You should come by the library, Steve. We have lots of new books in."

"I can't today," he told her. "I'm crafting armor."

"How exciting!" exclaimed Avery, "Are you planning an adventure?"

"You know me," Steve remarked. "I like to stay out of trouble and stick close to home."

"Sometimes people don't plan adventures, they just happen." Avery had read every adventure tale in the library; she loved those stories.

"That's true," Steve smiled at Avery. "But I'd rather just keep the armor in my inventory and read about adventures in books."

Steve crafted his iron armor. He tried it on

and walked around his house. "I must look like a warrior," he said to himself as he put the armor away and took a short walk before dusk. Steve would never venture out at night; he knew that was when creepers could attack him.

His farm wasn't far from the water, and he walked over and looked out at the enormous blue ocean as he wondered what lands might be on the other side. He had never hopped on a boat to find out.

If Steve had an adventure story to tell, it would be about the time he once tamed an ocelot. Lost in the vast, unexplored jungle, surrounded by bushes deep in the jungle biome, Steve spotted an animal racing past him toward an overgrown patch of grass and weeds. As the animal's pace slowed, he could make out its yellow fur covered in black and brownish spots. It was a wild ocelot!

The ocelot's piercing green eyes stared menacingly at Steve. Steve's heart skipped a beat. He wanted to tame this wild beast. He offered the feline raw fish, which the hungry ocelot eagerly accepted. With each bite, the ocelot transformed into a tame animal. Slowly the cat's skin took on a ginger tone until it resembled a typical tabby cat. The ocelot's tail shrunk, signifying it was no longer feral. Steve named the ocelot Snuggles. He'd be the first to admit he felt safer on the farm with Snuggles. As everyone knows, ocelots scare off creepers. Steve was afraid of creepers.

Steve knew that if you were careful, you could avoid running into any creepers, skeletons, spiders, silverfish, zombies, and other hostile mobs whose sole purpose was to attack. In fact, Steve had helped secure the village from a zombie attack. He built a fence all the way around the village and placed torches along the main street so all the land inside the wall was brightly lit day and night. This way he could be sure that zombies wouldn't spawn in his village. As Eliot the blacksmith mentioned, Steve had also built an Iron Golem to protect them. He placed iron blocks and a pumpkin on the ground and watched as the tough, mighty beast got to its feet. As Steve watched the monstrous stone creature lumber toward the village, he was sure it would be able to keep him and his villager friends safe from zombies and other mobs.

When he wasn't protecting his home from predators, Steve spent his time making coal out of wood. He traded the coal with Eliot the blacksmith for pickaxes, which he used for mining. He also traded his wheat for cookies from John the village farmer. When he mined for gold, he usually traded it for books with Avery the librarian. Between the villagers and the farm, he had all his needs provided for and a safe place to sleep every night. He loved coming back to the farm and hearing Snuggles meow as the ocelot relaxed in the greenery.

When night began to fall, Steve immediately got into his wool bed. Nighttime was the most vulnerable time; as the sun sank in the sky, the shadows grew and the well-lit areas became darker until Steve's village was the only place bright enough that the mobs wouldn't spawn there. But outside the walls, he could always hear the zombies groaning and the strange skittering sounds of spiders. If you weren't in your bed when night fell, you were pretty much an open target, but a well-built bed would keep you safe until daybreak. When dusk approached, Steve was always safely in his bed at the farm. Once Steve saw a tall, dark Enderman with a purple aura when he was out at dusk, but he knew not to stare. He safely made his escape and learned his lesson. When the lights began to dim, it was time to go home. There was no reason to take chances.

But that night as Steve slept in the comfort of his bed, he heard strange noises coming from the village. The villagers were in trouble, and as Steve listened to the groans and the sound of wood breaking, he knew it could only be one thing—a zombie attack! He tried to convince himself that he was just hearing things and they were fine. But the noises wouldn't stop. He imagined going into town and seeing the villagers turned into zombies, and he grabbed his clock to see how much time he had before morning. It was still so early; Steve clutched his clock tightly, wondering if he could wait until morning. But as he felt the clock tick in his hands and heard the villagers' cries, Steve knew he had to help right away. And since Eliot knew that Steve had the armor, he was probably waiting helplessly for Steve to attack the zombies.

The other villagers were also Steve's good friends. He liked villagers better than other explorers like him, because they couldn't be griefers and couldn't harm him. They had jobs and lived and worked together in the village, growing their crops and making useful things to trade. They followed predictable routines and never strayed far from home, but they helped one another and never caused any havoc in his life. Griefers were wanderers who spent their time playing pranks on other explorers and generally making trouble. They intentionally did bad things to other people to steal more stuff for themselves. There were some griefers who just picked on folks because they thought it was fun and they liked tricking people. They'd use TNT to destroy a house or lie and say they needed help and then attack. Steve didn't want to lose his house or his stuff to any griefers, so he was careful not to trust anyone but his villager friends. And now zombies were attacking them. Steve had to help.

He tried to convince himself that the Iron Golem could handle the zombies, but the desperate cries from the villagers meant the Golem wasn't powerful enough to defeat the zombies on its own. Or even worse, something had happened to the stone creature. Steve thought of Avery and the books he had gotten from her. He could imagine a zombie overpowering her as she raced through the streets in her flowing white robe. He wondered if the zombies were destroying John the farmer's crops. He imagined Eliot trying to hide in his blacksmith shop from the vicious monsters.

The cries grew louder and the images of his friends being attacked by zombies swirled around in his panicked mind. Steve knew he had to help them. If he didn't do something heroic soon, he would be a no-good coward who let the village get destroyed.

Although it defied all of his instincts to avoid danger, Steve threw off his covers and got out of bed. He checked the room for spiders and creepers, then went to his chest to get ready. For the first time, he suited up in all the armor he had made, which he loved having but never thought he'd use. Luckily Steve had a well-stocked inventory—since he never battled, he just collected armor—of swords and other tools to protect himself. He took out his compass, iron sword, bow, and arrows from his inventory. Then he paused and grabbed his special gold sword, just in case he needed it. His hands shook. His heart raced. He was scared. It was the moment Steve had always feared, and now he was living it.

utside Steve's house it was pitch dark, making it the perfect hour for hostile mobs to feast. The monsters had started to climb over the defensive wall surrounding the village and were swarming the buildings inside. Many of the torches Steve had placed throughout the village were gone. He saw a shallow pit in front of him and knew that a creeper must have exploded, destroying the lights and leaving the village in darkness. As Steve made his way out of his home, he gasped. A spider jockey was crawling up the wall of his house. The spider's red eyes glowed in the darkness as the skeleton sat on the aggressive arachnid. Steve knew that spider jockeys were rare and could destroy him in seconds. A spider's vision was excellent, and the skeleton was a skilled hunter, which made a spider jockey a double threat. Steve felt his heart beating through his armor-clad body. He reached for his bow and arrow and took a deep breath.

Within seconds, the skeleton spotted Steve and started to shoot. An arrow flew at Steve's chest but bounced off the armor. He sprinted away from the spider as it leapt from the wall toward him, and the skeleton's arrows came closer to Steve's unarmored legs. He ran as he narrowly avoided the arrows. Steve turned back and took aim at the spider but wasn't able to kill the dreaded enemy as fast as he hoped. As more arrows flew toward Steve, he dodged them swiftly. At the same time, he reloaded his bow and shot again at the spider. Steve knew it was important to kill the spider before the skeleton; if the spider were alone, without being weighed down by the bony skeleton, it could destroy him in an instant.

Steve slowed down, and with a clear eye, he shot an arrow at the spider. *Thunk!* It hit the spider right in its belly. The creature fell to the ground, and the skeleton launched a solo attack. With one more expert shot, Steve was able to take the skeleton down.

He had defeated the spider jockey! He had never beaten such a tough enemy before. He grabbed the eye dropped by the spider and put it in his inventory, knowing it could be useful later. Bursting with energy from the conquest of the spider jockey, Steve set off to the village to fight zombies with a bit more swagger in his step. Now he was a warrior.

As he approached the village, Eliot the blacksmith ran past him toward his shop.

"Help!" Eliot screamed. "You have the armor, you can beat the zombies."

Steve knew Eliot had faith in him, but did he realize how scared Steve was? Steve saw that a group of zombies surrounded a local village family, as they tried to open the door to their home. The villagers tried to shield themselves, but the green, vacant-eyed zombies tore doors from homes, shops, and restaurants. They shattered glass windows and ripped roofs from small homes. There was no place to hide. He wanted to follow Eliot back to his shop, but he knew hiding was a cowardly choice.

Steve looked for the pumpkin-headed Iron Golem. It was nowhere to be found. He walked over to a patch of grass. There he saw a large iron body broken on the ground. Its pumpkin head lay next to the slain Golem's mammoth feet. A griefer must have come into the village and killed it with the intention of harvesting its iron. But he had no time to come up with theories on what had happened to the Iron Golem. Steve had a sea of zombies racing toward him.

Seeking cover behind a large tree, he hoped he could hide from the zombies. Yet he wasn't safe; there was a group of them making a quick approach. Steve charged at them with his iron sword, destroying two instantly. After his battle with the spider jockey, he felt confident he'd win this fight quickly. He was wrong. Every minute, more zombies spawned. The injured zombies called for reinforcement, and Steve was quickly outnumbered. He knew his armor could protect him while he battled, but the sheer volume of zombies made him doubt that he could win. And Steve's swords were wearing out; his first iron sword had worn out and broken earlier in the fight, and now his last one was almost useless as well.

Steve worried about the villagers. What if he couldn't defeat the zombies? Would all the villagers be turned into zombie villagers? For all of the items Steve had saved, he didn't have a potion of weakness, and he didn't even have enough time to craft an Enchanted Golden Apple—the two items necessary to cure a zombie villager. Perhaps he could create an iron gate and put any zombie villagers behind it as a temporary jail. This would keep them from hurting him while he defeated the zombies. But time wasn't on Steve's side. He had to just keep fighting and hope he could figure out a way to save his villagers.

Steve went back into his inventory and switched to a bow and arrow. As he shot arrows at the zombies, he was able to knock out a few, but they had an army. His bow and arrow was no match for a platoon of the walking dead. Steve needed another plan. He thought of leading the zombies to the ocean or a cliff, as he knew they weren't too smart, and he could probably trick them into running right off a cliff or drowning. He wasn't even sure if zombies could drown, though, and he was trapped in the village, anyway, with these bloodthirsty zombies who were quickly outnumbering the villagers. To make matters worse, each villager who succumbed to a zombie attack instantly transformed into a zombie villager. Steve saw the village butcher, still dressed in his white apron but now turned monstrously green and rotten, pushing at another zombie at the back of the crowd that continued to attack him. Steve's old villager friends were now zombies, ready to destroy the one person who was trying to save and protect them. It was a losing battle! Steve took a chance and raced toward the zombies. He shot at them with his bow, taking them down quickly so they didn't have a chance to call in reinforcements. Just when he thought he had won the battle, he saw one more zombie in the distance.

As the lone zombie walked toward Steve, he shook in sheer terror. He had had enough excitement for one night, and despite his heroics, he was still scared. His hand quivered while he fumbled with the bow. He could barely shoot an arrow. When he finally did, the arrow traveled slowly through the air and fell next to the zombie. The arrow crunched beneath the zombie's feet as he closed in on Steve. Steve felt his heart beating in his chest, but he couldn't let fear dominate his desire to save his friends.

Then Steve heard Eliot the blacksmith call for help. He knew a zombie must be cornering Eliot. Steve couldn't let him down. He needed courage and strength.

Steve put away the bow and arrow and grabbed the most powerful gold sword from his inventory. He cradled the sword with his fist, but the powerful zombie grabbed the sword from Steve's hands and snapped the weapon in half. It dropped the sword on the grass and reached for Steve. With no time left to get a weapon from his inventory, he was defenseless. Steve began to sprint away from the enormous green-eyed creature of the night.

He raced through the familiar streets of the village, ran into Eliot's blacksmith shop, and slammed the door behind him. He figured that if he traded emeralds, he could get a new sword to defeat the zombie. But it was too late! Eliot the blacksmith was defeated and was spawning into a zombie. He had failed his friend. Steve was devastated and felt useless.

Eliot was turning into a zombie, and Steve stood and stared in fear at his friend. Steve was heartbroken. He had spent so much time trading and talking with Eliot, but he was now an enemy. He could hear Avery the librarian calling for help in the distance. He'd already let one villager friend down; he couldn't let it happen again. Steve had to get to Avery's library.

Thud! Crack! He heard the door being ripped apart by the menacing zombie. He plotted an escape. Steve grabbed a pickaxe from his inventory and dug a hole in the ground. As he dug deeper, he could hear the door being ripped from its hinges. Once the zombie stepped foot in the shop, Steve crawled out through the bottom of the shop and into the center of town. Emerging from the hole, he was cornered by a gang of zombies. Somehow Steve was able to weave his way through the zombies and run out of the village, but the zombie mob followed closely behind. Avery's cries grew louder, and Steve knew he had to return to the village, but it was impossible.

Looking back, he could see the zombies were close behind. He shot arrows while he ran, striking a few of his enemies. As he made his way through the dark night, he tried to find a place to hide, but then he was cornered. He could make out a cave in the distance. Although Steve was terrified of caves and had never been in one before, he was hoping he could hide there or find lava to attack the horde of zombies. They were getting closer, so Steve ran faster toward the cave.

One zombie was inches from Steve's back. As it stepped closer, Steve trembled with fear, accidently letting his chest plate fall off. Steve tried to pick it up, but with a strong grasp, the zombie yanked the plate from Steve's hands and put the armored plate on its own chest. The zombie called out to his gang. The chest plate transformed this ordinary zombie into an even more powerful zombie, since he was armored and couldn't be attacked. He also had an armored helmet, which meant, unlike other zombies, he could live in daylight, although the others would burn in the sun.

The armored zombie leapt at Steve. He jumped back. Unarmored, Steve knew there was one only way to escape. He'd spent the morning mining, and he had run into an area with lava and water, so he had enough obsidian in his bag to make a frame. He quickly stacked the jet black blocks together. As he lit them on fire, a purple mist rose through the air. Steve's portal to the Nether was complete. With a glance back at his village, Steve turned and made his escape from the zombie attack and into the Nether.

3

DOWN THE HOLE

Steve drifted weightlessly until he landed in the red landscape of the Nether. Filled with lava pools, the Nether didn't track time with day and night like the Overworld. Steve looked at his compass to find his direction, only to see the needle on the compass go in circles. Compasses and clocks were useless in the Nether.

As he adjusted to the crimson glow from the Nether, Steve cautiously explored his new landscape. This was unlike any place Steve had ever been, and his eyes had to adjust to the new lighting. The Nether was dangerous, but it was also filled with many useful resources. Mushrooms sprouted from the ground, and Steve saw a lava pool in the distance. Steve leaned over to pick a mushroom and knew that the fermented spider's eye he had from the jockey spider mixed with sugar could create a potion.

Before he could grab his first mushroom, he heard the high-pitched sounds of a ghast. Its white boxy body with tentacles floated by with its eyes closed.

Steve quickly surveyed the area for a good hiding place. Stepping too close to the lava pool would kill him, and there were no trees to hide behind or scary caves to provide shelter as the ghast passed Steve. Ghasts had limited vision and couldn't see him if he hid behind some leaves or glass, but there was nothing in sight. Another option was going back through the portal, but then he'd have to face the armored zombie. Also, he couldn't go back to the village until he had a plan to save Avery the librarian, the other villagers, and himself. He tried to remain quiet, hoping the ghast would float by, but it was too late. The ghast saw Steve, opened its demonic red eyes, and readied itself for an attack.

The ghast looked like a jellyfish with white tentacles sprouting from its underbelly. It made a chirping noise signaling it was attacking. Without armor or a sword, Steve was defenseless and had no way to shield the attack. The ghast's cavernous mouth opened wide as a red-hot fireball emerged. The flames glistened as the fireball rushed through the breezy Nether sky. Steve didn't have time to dodge the fiery mess. With a single throw of his fist, he hit the fireball and redirected it toward the ghast. The ghast let out a pained wail as it exploded.

Steve made his way through the Nether and walked past a lava waterfall until he came to a patch of Soul Sand. While collecting the blocks of sand, he could see a Nether fortress in the distance past a large field of lava. Suddenly Steve had an idea! Diamonds could be found in a Nether fortress. If Steve obtained diamonds, he could craft a powerful diamond sword to attack the armored zombie.

"I will use forty diamonds," Steve said, although he was all alone and had nobody to talk to. He missed his conversations with Eliot the Blacksmith, and it comforted him to simply hear words out loud, even if nobody was listening.

He paused, and with great hope he exclaimed, "And with those diamonds, I will create the most powerful sword in the world. I will use it to slay that armored zombie and help the villagers!"

"Diamonds?" A voice called out, and Steve realized he wasn't alone.

"Who are you?" asked Steve.

"I'm Jack," the voice replied, and he came out from behind blocks. He wore blue diamond armor.

"Wow, you have diamond armor." Steve was impressed. He was also wary of this stranger. He could be a griefer. But Steve was lonely and wanted company.

"If you give me an iron ingot, I can teach you how to travel in the void," said Jack.

The void was an area in the Nether that had no hostile mobs. Steve had heard that it was a safe way to travel through this scary land.

"For just one iron ingot?" Steve was shocked—that was a small request for such an enormous task.

"Yes," Jack said as Steve gave him the ingot.

Suddenly Jack took out a diamond sword and leapt toward Steve. Steve jumped back.

"I want everything in your inventory," demanded Jack. "Now!"

The blue sword glistened in the dark red Nether. Steve sprinted toward a lava pool, but he couldn't escape. It was either drown in hot lava or be destroyed by Jack's sword.

Suddenly Jack and Steve heard a chirping sound. It was a ghast. It fired at them, Jack ran to avoid the flame, accidently pushing Steve away, and Jack tripped into a pool of lava. Steve wanted to grab the diamond sword from Jack the griefer but was too late, as it was already covered in lava. To even reach for the tip of the handle could result in Steve being burned or destroyed. He also didn't have time to get it since he had a ghast attacking him.

Steve quickly exchanged his sword for a bow and arrow, and with one hit, he knocked out the ghast.

"Gotcha!" Steve shouted as the ghast was destroyed. Then he looked around nervously, remembering the last time he had shouted out loud. He was scared another griefer would come, and he needed to be prepared.

Steve had encountered his first griefer and had walked away alive. With the victories over the ghasts, he was beginning to feel confident as he walked across a Nether bridge over a sea of lava. He passed enormous columns made of Nether brick that seemed to stretch as far as the sky. Small fires burned on the ground, and he jumped to avoid them. He paid close attention to the ground beneath his feet, because he never knew what he might encounter in the Nether. He made his way toward the Nether fortress and was hopeful that he could find diamonds and save his friends.

As he jumped over a small pool of lava, a zombie pigman leapt out, ready to attack Steve. The pink pig with a box-shaped head and rotting flesh was armed with a sword and in attack mode.

I can't seem to shake zombies! Steve thought as he deftly built a three brick wall to shield him from the zombie pigman. Then he jumped up high and knocked the zombie pigman to the ground. This attack spawned a group of zombie pigmen, all ready to attack Steve. Using cobblestone blocks, he constructed a booth with four walls and mined a hole in the bottom of the booth. He used the blocks to strike the zombie pigmen. As each zombie was defeated, it dropped gold ingots. Steve quickly collected the ingots and crafted them into a sword.

Touting his new sword, Steve made his escape toward the Nether fortress to find his diamonds. Flying above the Fortress and aiming for Steve was a blaze. Its yellow body and black eyes flew above the Fortress and shot at Steve as it guarded this majestic fortress made of Nether block. Steve grabbed a Nether block to shield himself from the fiery blows the blaze was unleashing on him.

The blaze spawned! Two more blazes appeared. Both fired at him. The flames landed incredibly close to his body, almost burning his new gold sword. A blaze dropped a blaze rod by his feet. Steve picked it up, knowing it was helpful when brewing potions. Steve barely missed another blast. He knew the only way to survive this clash with the blazes was to craft an Enchanted Golden Apple. He had been planning on crafting an Enchanted Golden Apple when he returned to the village to cure Eliot the blacksmith, but he had to use it now. Enchanted Golden Apples also had the power to shield people from fire for five minutes, and at that moment Steve was being blasted with heat. Enchanted Golden Apples were expensive to craft, but as flames flew at Steve's body, it was his only option. Steve crafted an Enchanted Golden Apple with gold blocks and an apple from his inventory, then he ate it all in one bite, saved from the fire for five minutes.

It was a race against the clock as he battled the three blazes that were now standing in front of the fortress. Their power was diminished due to the Enchanted Golden Apple, but they were still skilled as they tried to smash Steve to the ground. Steve unleashed his mighty iron sword and destroyed the blazes, collecting the points the blazes dropped after he defeated them. With the glow of a victory, Steve entered the grand fortress.

The Fortress walls were decorated with glowstone blocks. The yellow light emanating from the slabs seemed to reflect off the Nether blocks and light the room. The ambiance gave the Fortress a feeling of being both grand and cozy. Steve had never seen anything so beautiful. He quickly eyed for any blazes that might be spawning in the fortress, but he didn't see any around. He knew ghasts couldn't survive in a Nether fortress, because ghasts couldn't survive in enclosed places and the buildings were made of materials that could withstand a ghast blast. This enabled Steve to relax and soak in the awesomeness of this grand fortress. In the center of an interior room, Steve saw an enormous staircase made of Nether bricks with Soul Sand, and Nether wart was growing on the ground on both sides of the staircase.

Steve walked down the staircase and reached over to pick up the Nether wart, which was an essential ingredient to have when making potions. As he reached to pick up his first batch, a blaze emerged from behind a wall. Steve mined a Nether block, covering himself with the flame-resistant block as he plunged his sword into the blaze and watched it fall to the floor in agony.

The minute the blaze died, a dark red and brown cube jumped from a lava pool to the center of the staircase. Its eyes looked like flames, and for a second Steve was mesmerized. He had never seen a magma cube before, and the intensity of its eyes held Steve's attention. Of course, he knew the magma cube was hostile, and he had to defeat it. With a swift blow from his sword, the magma cube fell back and split in two. Steve jumped toward the multiple cubes and struck each one until they were killed. Magma cream oozed from the cube and Steve ran to pick it up due to its value in the Nether.

With his eyes peeled for hostile mobs, Steve walked through the fortress in search of the rare diamonds. The rooms were empty. Another explorer must have been in the fortress before him and emptied it of its treasures. He could see blazes spawning in a room as Steve rushed from the fortress back into the wide-open Nether. He hoped to find another fortress to get diamonds.

Steve could only see lava ponds and fires. It could take him days to find another fortress, and his food bar was getting very low. He couldn't continue searching in the Nether. He had to make his way back to the Overworld, where he could hunt for cows to fill his food bar. He also couldn't return to the portal he used to get to the Nether, because it would bring him back into the zombie attack. Steve had to make another portal, which meant he'd land in a foreign land. This frightened Steve, but it was his only option.

Steve constructed the frame using more of

the obsidian from his bag. He set it on fire and leapt into the portal. He had no idea where he'd wind up when he stepped out. Steve missed his wheat farm and Snuggles's meows. He hoped that his home and his ocelot would still be there when he returned to the Overworld. He secretly feared he'd never make his way back. As he transported between the two worlds, he closed his eyes and pretended he was in his old comfy wool bed.

4
TREASURE HUNTERS IN THE TEMPLE

Steve opened his eyes and saw dust. well, it wasn't exactly dust. It was sand, and it seemed to go on forever. He was in a desert far from the familiarity of his wheat farm and the village. Steve was worried about finding food. It seemed like a barren wasteland. There was nothing. He had heard about people ending up in the desert, finding mirages, and getting lost in the expanse. He could build a house with sandstone blocks or mine. Worried that he was low on food bars, he walked through the desert in search of anything.

The tan blocks were almost blinding. Stairs were built out of bricks of sand. He stood high atop a stack of blocks to see if there was a village in the distance, but there wasn't. Steve thought this was the end. He was going to die and be respawned back in the wheat farm. If that happened, zombies would probably just attack him in his home. He trudged along the sandy streets of the desert hoping he'd see some life.

When he had given up hope, Steve started to mine. If he could get a bunch of sandstone blocks, he would be able to build a house and start a new life in this desolate world. He used his pickaxe and got deep beneath the surface. After mining for a while, he came upon an enormous square. It was a temple! He knew that was where treasure could be found. Maybe he could find his diamonds. Steve dug a hole into the center of this desert temple. The temple looked like an Egyptian pyramid. As he entered the temple, he heard some voices. He wasn't alone.

"Who's here?" Steve screamed with a quiver in his tone. But there was no response. He could hear people whispering, and he was worried that he would be attacked.

"Who are you?" Steve called out again. Utter silence.

Suddenly, three people emerged from behind a sandstone wall—two boys and a girl.

"Don't tell him, Henry," a boy with dyed blue leather armor and a blue helmet yelled at his friend, who stood holding a pickaxe and wearing gold armor and a gold helmet.

"Max, everyone knows the only reason people go into temples is to find the four treasure chests," Henry told his friend with the blue helmet.

"You have to trust him," chimed in their third friend with pink leather armor and a pink helmet.

"Lucy, why should we?" Henry sounded annoyed.

"Are you treasure hunters?" Steve questioned the group. After encountering the griefer in the Nether, he was suspicious of everyone.

"Maybe," Henry said with an attitude.

"Are you alone?" Max asked Steve.

"Yes," he replied, hoping they weren't griefers planning to ruin his day or even kill him. But he didn't have anything too valuable on him, because he had spent all his gold on the Enchanted Golden Apple, and Steve was close to starving.

He looked over at this gang of three, and realized that he was going to have to trust and join them. He had no other choice.

"How are you planning on getting the treasure? You know it's trapped," said Steve.

"Of course we know that! We're experts," said Henry.

"Do you want in? We can split the loot,"

Lucy offered.

"If you're experts, why do you need my help?" Steve was suspicious.

"Because we feel sorry for you," Lucy smiled.

"Our motto is the more the merrier. We love making new friends," said Max.

Henry looked at his friends. "Maybe we should just leave him alone. He may be a griefer. How can we trust him?"

"He seems nice," said Lucy.

"How do you know he seems nice?" Henry was shocked. "We just met him."

"You're right, he could be a griefer, but he seems scared of us," Lucy said to defend herself.

"True, but that could be an act. He could be a cunning griefer." Henry never trusted anybody, but there weren't a lot of people who trusted Henry.

"Well, there's only one way we can find out if he is a griefer. We have to let him work with us," said Max.

"Where are you from?" Henry asked Steve.

"I live on a wheat farm by a village. I left when it was being attacked by zombies," Steve told the group.

"A wheat farm?" Lucy questioned.

"It's not just a wheat farm. I also grow carrots, potatoes, and pumpkins, and I breed pigs."

"Carrots?" Henry's eyes beamed. Carrots were extremely valuable, and Henry knew Steve must have lots of resources on the farm. That meant Steve was valuable.

"Yes, I have a large house." Steve didn't want to sound like he was bragging, but he was proud of his property. He had more than six bedrooms and multiple beds. He had food that could serve several users. He had worked hard to get all of this, but he stopped himself from saying too much. He had seen the glint in Henry's eye, and he didn't like it.

"Do you have extra rooms in your house?" Lucy asked Steve.

"Yes, I have six," Steve replied and added for no reason in particular, "I also have an ocelot named Snuggles."

"That's nice." Lucy nodded her head.

"If we let you join us, will you take us to your wheat farm?" Henry asked with a smile.

"Yes, but I'm afraid it may be taken over by zombies. When I was helping the local villagers, I dropped my armor, and now there is an armed zombie on the loose."

"Armed zombies are super powerful," said Max.

"I know!" Steve agreed.

"We will help you slay the zombie," said

Henry.

"I have a plan," Steve said. He realized he couldn't battle the zombies alone, and since he had nothing for these guys to steal, he had to trust them. He needed help. So he told the gang his plan to find forty diamonds and craft the most powerful sword.

"That's a genius idea," Lucy smiled.

"We want in," said Henry.

"Why?" Steve couldn't shake his suspicions.

"Our home was destroyed, and we'd rather hunt for treasures than build a house. If we lived on your wheat farm, we could go on endless treasure hunts collecting jewels," Henry told Steve.

"And Max is an expert fighter," Lucy added. "So you really want him on your side."

-"Okay!" Steve replied. He was going to trust these new people—he was going to make new friends—but suddenly, as he walked further into the temple, he realized he might be stepping into a booby trap.

Watch out!" screamed lucy.

Steve looked down as he almost fell into the temple's chamber. As he looked at the ground, he saw nine blocks of TNT and colored wool.

"That's the pressure plate," Max told Steve. "You've never been in a temple before, have you?"

"No," said Steve humbly, "I've never traveled further than the village by my wheat farm until now. Since the zombie attack, I've been to the Nether—"

Max interrupted, "You survived the Nether?!"

"How impressive!" said Lucy respectfully.

"I've been everywhere," Henry said quite confidently. "And I'll show you the ropes. First thing, don't step on a pressure plate, or you'll be a goner."

"We have to dig around it." Lucy showed Steve, and they all started to dig deep underneath the temple in search of the four treasure chests.

"I hope these treasure chests have diamonds, and we can use them to build the sword," Steve said. He was excited.

"We can't talk about what we'll find. We have to concentrate on getting there. This takes a lot of skill," said Max.

"Let's take the wool and the TNT from the booby trap," suggested Lucy.

"Good idea!" said Henry. "It's valuable and it's also fun to blow stuff up."

"Henry!" Lucy was upset as she continued, "It's not about blowing stuff up. It's about finding the treasure."

Steve loved listening to their banter. He had spent so much time alone, and now he understood the importance of friends, especially other explorers and adventurers such as himself. These new friends could help Steve—they made sure he didn't walk on the pressure plate—unlike the villagers. Steve was able to help them, but they could never reciprocate, because they were defenseless and couldn't battle hostile mobs.

The group mined their way past the pit, descending with a splash. They landed in a chamber. Steve looked up and saw flames burning on the torches lining the walls of the chamber. As they made their way through the belly of the temple, they looked carefully for booby traps and moved slowly around this foreign landscape.

"We are getting closer to the treasure!" exclaimed Max.

"We have to be careful," explained Henry. "If we set off the TNT, not only will we die, we'll blow up the four treasure chests and destroy the loot."

Steve was impressed with Henry's treasure hunting skills. The group slowly mined their way into the secret chamber and made sure they didn't set off explosions. As they banged their pickaxes against the temple walls, the sandstone bricks crumbled at their feet. They walked into a large tan room filled with bricks of sandstone and four holes in a group. Henry approached the first hole, and the group followed closely behind. It was empty! The other two holes were also empty. They finally made their way to the final hole, and they found a treasure chest.

"Stand back!" Henry warned the group.

The group stood against the wall. "What's wrong, Henry?" asked Max.

"I don't trust it. Why would somebody leave one treasure chest? That makes no sense," explained Henry.

"You think it's a booby trap?" asked Lucy.

"I'm not sure, and I'm not willing to risk it. I think we should leave it," said Henry.

"Henry's right." Max stood next to his friend as he said, "If we open it and it's loaded with TNT, it could explode and we'd be killed."

Steve wondered if being killed was all that bad. He'd respawn in his bed, and this would all be a distant memory. Then Steve remembered the zombies.

"I want to check for diamonds," Steve told the group.

"It's not worth it," said Max.

"But I need those forty diamonds. I have to save the village. I need the powerful sword," he cried out.

"I know you want that sword, but this isn't the way you're going to get it. This will only end badly," Lucy comforted him.

"We've done this before. We know how bad it could get," Henry informed Steve.

"Also, diamonds are a rare find. If we open the chest and it doesn't explode, it's most likely rotten flesh and gold," Lucy said. She wanted Steve to know the reality of treasure hunting.

Steve walked over to the treasure chest.

"Stop!" Lucy screamed at him. "A griefer could have rigged it to explode!"

Max looked at his compass. "Everyone keep

track of where we are at the moment, in case we get killed. We need to know where to find each other."

"I have my coordinates," Lucy told the group.

"Dude, you think I'm stupid enough to open it? I'm not like you guys—I don't like to get killed," Steve defended himself. "Why don't *you* open the treasure chest?"

"We don't take stupid risks. Nobody would leave one treasure chest unless a griefer with mod was creating glitches and trying to hurt someone," said Henry.

Steve wondered how Henry knew so much about griefers.

"Let's get out of here. I think there's another temple nearby that might have treasure," Henry told the group.

"Let's follow this map. Take out your compasses," Lucy said. Before they could make their escape, the ground broke beneath them and they were falling, uncertain of where they might land.

6
DUNGEONS AND EXPLOSIONS

Thump! The gang landed on the ground in a dark room. "Where are we?" asked Steve with a shaky voice.

"Where's Max?" asked Henry nervously.

Suddenly Max flew down and landed next to them. He was carrying a torch.

"I grabbed this on the way down," he told the gang.

"Smart," said Lucy. "Let's take a look around."

The light from the torch helped the group navigate through the dark halls of the dungeon. A piston came from the wall and blew out the torch. They tried to weave their way through dungeon's tunnels using the light coming from the hole above them. Each step they took seemed like an eternity. Not being able to see in the dark made them nervous.

"What's that?" Lucy pointed to a light

coming from the wall. "Maybe it's an exit!"

The light had a fiery reddish glow. It vanished.

"The light is over there now," Henry said. He tried to point, but it was useless. They couldn't see their feet in front of them.

Max called out, "I see it over here!"

Steve's voice began to crack when he said, "It's not a light. It's spiders!"

Spider eyes lined the walls of the dungeon. Max rushed toward a spider and hit it with a mighty blow from his sword. The spider was killed. Max's hit was so powerful that it made a hole in the wall, and a small beam of light shined in the room.

As Max turned around, he could see a zombie lurking in the corner near his friends. "Watch out!" he warned them.

Steve took out his iron sword and killed the zombie instantly.

"There are more!" exclaimed Lucy. Four zombies spawned, emerging from the dark corners of the creepy dungeon as the walls continued to fill with spiders. Their eyes lit up the room. The light that emanated from the hole in the wall wasn't enough to help the treasure hunters see or ward away hostile mobs that feed off users of the night.

"We're trapped," said Lucy breathlessly as

she killed her tenth spider.

Steve charged at the zombies while Max tried to slay the many spiders that leapt from the walls. A spider jumped on Max, but he brushed it off with a blow from his fist and finished it with his sword.

No matter how many zombies and spiders the team of four was able to destroy, they couldn't stop this invasion of hostile mobs. They were outnumbered.

Lucy hit a spider with all of her strength, making a gaping hole on the side of the dungeon wall. Lava began to trickle down the side of the wall. She banged harder, and the stream of lava increased. Henry made his way over to Lucy and started to hit the wall with his pickaxe.

"Why are you wasting your time breaking down the wall?" asked Steve, annoyed that he was left alone to handle a swarm of zombies that were overwhelming him—until he saw the lava quickly flowing through the crack in the wall.

"We need to flood this room with lava," explained Henry.

"Use your pickaxes and make a hole in the wall where we saw the light!" he told the others.

As Max and Steve pickaxed an escape tunnel, Lucy and Henry created a waterfall of lava that rushed through the dungeon. Lucy and Henry raced toward the tunnel. The lava rushed behind them as they ran faster to avoid being burned by the hot lava.

They made it! Steve looked back to see the spiders' red eyes swallowed up by hot orange lava streaming through the dungeon and drowning the evil night-crawling zombies and spiders.

The treasure hunters made their escape to the secret chamber. Henry ran toward the blue wool and grabbed TNT.

"What are you going to do with that?" Steve was shocked that Henry had explosives.

"What do you think? I'm going to blow this place up! It's filled with hostile mobs and it doesn't even have treasure."

They made their way up the sandstone steps, passed through the large doors, and swiftly exited the temple. Outside the temple doors, Henry placed the TNT next to a redstone torch. As they sprinted toward the sandy terrain, the temple exploded. Boom! The temple burst into flames. A large cloud of smoke lingered in the air as rubble from the temple shot high above their heads. The friends shielded themselves from the debris. The temple walls piled around the structure and left an outline of where this temple, once home to a treasure trove, stood in the barren Minecraft desert.

7

CAVES, STORMS, AND OTHER THREATS

Steve had to admit the thrill of running out of the desert temple and watching it burst into flames was exhilarating, but he knew this wasn't the life he wanted. He yearned to leave and return to the village. He needed to find those diamonds fast.

"We need to leave the desert," announced Steve.

"We're treasure hunters. We live in the desert," his new friends told him.

"But it's impossible to live here," protested Steve.

"You'll get used to it." Lucy patted Steve on the back.

"I thought you wanted to go back to the wheat farm with me," said Steve.

"We'd like to visit, but we love hunting treasure," said Henry.

Steve loved his new friends, but he also missed his home. He knew it was just a matter of time before he had to make a decision—was he going to stay with them or go back home? As they walked, Steve could see some greenery in the distance.

"Look, Steve, you got your wish," said Henry. "It looks like the desert ends here."

"I see a meadow," Steve said as he pointed at a green patch of land.

"And a cave!" Max was excited. "Let's go mining!"

"We don't have enough food," warned Steve. "When you go mining, you're supposed to also bring a bucket of water and pickaxes. Do we even have enough food bars? I'm really hungry."

Steve's food bar was almost depleted. He needed to go back to the wheat farm.

"Lucy is a skilled hunter. She can get you anything you want," said Henry.

Lucy said, "I'll get us a pig to eat. You can't give up now Steve. You need to go home with that diamond sword."

Pigs were in the meadow, and Lucy took out her bow and arrow. She struck the pigs. "Now we can feast," she announced to her friends.

"Thanks," Steve said as his food bar filled.

"Trust us, Steve," Henry said as he pointed them in the direction of the cave. "We need to mine in the cave. I promise you it will be fun. Just get some equipment from your inventory.

Don't be afraid to use it."

"You seem like a hoarder," Max laughed.

"A what?" Steve was confused.

"You save everything but never want to use it. I bet you have an insane amount of pickaxes and super awesome swords," said Max.

"Last time I used my armor, I dropped it and a zombie stole it. That's how I got into this mess in the first place," explained Steve.

"Yeah, that must have stunk," said Henry. "But think about the plus side. If you had never lost that armor and gone through the portal, you would have never met us. And if you want to find diamonds, you're going to have to mine in a cave near lava."

"Yeah lava and diamonds are usually found in the same caves," added Lucy.

"But lava kills," warned Steve.

"You want to beat the zombies and save the village?" asked Henry.

"Yes, I do!" Steve replied as he grabbed his pickaxe and tried to hide the fear of his first cave mining expedition.

"You will, Steve, if you stick with us," Henry said confidently.

"Let's go find diamonds in the cave!" Lucy was excited to mine.

The cave was dark, but it wasn't as scary as Steve imaged. The ceilings were low, and the team stuck together as they used their pickaxes to dig deep within the cavern. Steve couldn't hear any hostile mobs, and he began to relax and enjoy this exploration.

"Do you hear that?" asked Lucy.

"Sounds like water," replied Max as he banged his pickaxe against the dark cave floor.

"It could also be lava," said Henry.

"Diamonds!" Steve shouted out as he used all of his energy to dig through the cave floor. The gang began to collect coal, iron, and gold.

"Let's not get carried away," Henry said. Then he quickly screamed, "Watch out!"

A cave spider slipped through a hole in the wall of the cave. They knew it had a poisonous bite, and they had to kill it.

"We have to break the spawner," Max told the group. "It's the only way to stop it."

Cobwebs filled the cave, and the walls were crawling with spiders. "Ouch!" Henry called out.

"Henry's been bitten," Lucy screamed.

"I have milk in my inventory!" Steve announced and ran over to him. Steve handed him the milk and said, "Drink this, it will help you feel better."

Henry drank the milk. Milk helped lessen the effects of the cave spider's poisonous bite, and his health bar increased.

"And we made fun of you for being a hoarder," Lucy smiled. "If we didn't have that milk, Henry might have—" She stopped herself. If Henry had died, he would have gone back to the spawn point, and he may never have found his way back to the group.

"We have to stop the spiders," Henry said weakly as he sipped the milk.

"Lucky for you, Steve had milk," Max said as he suffocated a spider that crept up on him.

"Hold it down for six seconds," Henry told Max, "or it won't die. These spiders are tricky."

"Get a torch, Max," ordered Lucy. "They hate light."

"I have one of those in my inventory!" Steve grabbed a torch.

"Being prepared helps!" Lucy exclaimed. "And you, my friend, are very prepared."

Steve walked through the cave with a torch, placing it on a wall. The light revealed the severity of the spider attack. It seemed as if the cave were wallpapered with spiders that spawned by the second. Max picked up a handful of gravel and threw it on the spiders, destroying a cluster that crawled by his feet.

Steve began to build a wall.

"Steve, it's not a time to build," Henry said weakly.

"I'm not building. I'm saving us!" Steve

grabbed bricks. "Come closer to me. Max, please carry Henry over here."

The friends came closer to Steve as he quickly built a wall, which trapped the spiders as the group made an exit from the cave.

"Steve you saved us," said Henry with a smile. "You're the master builder."

"And I'm the master hunter," Lucy quickly added.

"I'm a master sword fighter," boasted Max.

"And what am I?" Henry joked with the group.

"You're the master griefer," said Max, and Henry shot him a dirty look.

"What?" Steve asked in shock.

"He was just kidding," Henry replied.

"Everyone knows you're the master treasure hunter, Henry. You always plan the great strategies for getting our treasures," said Lucy.

"Yes, that's what I am," said Henry proudly. He stood up in front of the crowd as if he were accepting an award. "I am the master treasure hunter."

"Who gets bitten by cave spiders," said Max slyly.

"That's not funny." Henry pushed Max playfully.

Lucy smiled at the group. "It's nice that we all have roles."

"Together we will make the most powerful team," added Henry.

Suddenly Steve dodged an arrow that flew too close to his head. "Unless they get us first!" Steve said.

"Skeletons!" shouted Max, and a new battle was about to begin.

8
SKELETONS

It sounded like a parade of rattling bones as the skeletons raced toward them with great force and shot arrows from a hill high above the fearless foursome. One skeleton leapt down, and Max charged toward it with his sword. His powerful blow ripped the head off the skeleton. This infuriated the other skeletons, and they shot arrows as fast at they could.

An arrow flew through the air, and Henry fell back.

"Are you hit?" asked Lucy.

"It hit my arm," Henry said as he got up and shot an arrow with his other hand. "It hurts, but I'll be okay."

Henry's health level was still low from the spider bite, and now it dipped even lower as he was attacked. The battle was making him weaker.

Steve knocked out two skeletons with his sword. When three skeletons surrounded him, he struck one with his sword. The other two had their bows pointed at Steve. He realized this might be the end. After all the battles, he would be killed, spawned back in his village, and still unable to help the villagers. His heart was heavy, and he was about to surrender. Suddenly, Lucy and Max crept up behind the skeletons and knocked them to the ground with their swords.

"There are so many of them," Lucy said as she looked at the countless skeletons that approached the group. The night sky began to darken. The black skeleton eyes seemed almost invisible in the charcoal-colored night.

"We need to find shelter," said Steve as a skeleton came up behind him and knocked him to the ground. Steve got up and struck the skeleton.

Two pairs of purple eyes shone through the sea of skeletons.

"It's Endermen," Lucy called to Steve. "Don't stare at them."

But it was too late, and the Endermen were provoked. They teleported, landing in the thick of the skeleton battle.

"There's water down here," said Lucy as she ran up the hill to flee from the skeletons. "We need to jump and swim."

"Get a bucket of water," shouted Henry.

"I have that in my inventory!" Steve yelled

to the group, but it was too late. Lucy was trapped.

"I can't," Lucy cried out as the two Endermen teleported in front of her.

A skeleton cornered Steve. Max swung his sword into the skeleton's head, killing it and saving Steve. But there were still six more skeletons left to battle. The foursome was weak, and their health and food bars were low. It was just minutes before it became a losing battle.

The Endermen surrounded Lucy. "Help!" she called to her friends.

Steve could see Lucy battling the beasts with her sword, but the blows didn't weaken the Endermen. He saw her jump off the cliff into the water. The two Endermen dove in after her and plunged to their deaths.

As Lucy came out of the water, purple eyes emerged from the distance. More Endermen approached.

"This is never-ending!" she said as she jumped back in the water. The Endermen followed, succumbing to the same fate as the previous Endermen.

A creeper lurked in the darkness. It crept toward Max. Its green body came closer to Max as Lucy screamed out from the water, "Watch out, Max, it's a creeper!"

"There's one behind you, too!" Henry called to Lucy as she stood at the edge of the water.

The stealthy green monsters had a talent for silently creeping up behind players and unleashing an attack that left both the creeper and the player defeated.

Lucy ran as fast as she could toward Steve, Henry, and Max. With her sword out, she attacked the skeletons that battled her friends. The skeletons lunged at the group. The friends used all their might to battle these creatures of the night, and the gang pierced the bony beasts with their swords.

"If only we had the powerful diamond sword, this battle would be easier," Steve said as his sword hit a skeleton.

"Do you hear that?" Lucy asked the group.

The sound of a fuse being burnt emanated from the creepers. Something was going to explode! The group ran as the creepers moved toward the skeletons. Boom! The creepers exploded and disintegrated after an attack on the skeletons. Three CDs appeared where the skeletons fell. Steve grabbed the discs as Lucy and Max battled the remaining skeletons.

"When we get the diamonds for the sword, we'll also use some to make a jukebox. When we get back to my wheat farm, we'll have a huge party to celebrate our victory."

The gang cheered, but before they could rejoice, an arrow flung at the group! "More skeletons!" They collectively moaned as the group spotted more Endermen approaching them.

"How are we going to get out of this one?" Steve asked as he held the CDs tightly in his hand. He didn't want the group to see his hand shaking because he was nervous.

Suddenly, a loud boom echoed through the night sky. It was thunder. As raindrops began to fall, the Endermen retreated, and the skillful fighter Max was able to defeat the last skeleton. The sounds of rain hitting the blocks had a calming effect on the group, who were weary from battle.

"We should find some shelter," Steve said as rain dripped from his body.

"Look at our pile of bones," Max showed the group proudly. "We might have had a difficult battle, but we gained lots of experience, and now we can use these bones."

"I hope we don't run into wolves," said Lucy.

"But now we can tame them," Max held a bone.

"Wolves scare off Endermen," added Steve.

A chicken came into view and Lucy hunted it and explained, "We need to get our food bars full."

The rain stopped, and the group sat and ate. They tried to relax as they kept one eye open for hostile mobs.

"We need to find diamonds," said Steve.

"Maybe we should stop looking for the diamonds. I want to hunt for treasure," Henry said as he ate the chicken and watched his food and health bars increase.

"I need to save my village. I'm their only hope," Steve said. He was angry.

"It doesn't matter if you don't go home. Hunting treasure is much better and a lot more fun," Henry lashed out.

"What about our party?" Steve held the discs.

"It sounds like fun, but I want to get treasure," protested Henry.

"I thought you guys were going to help me find the diamonds," Steve said to the group. "I thought you wanted to be a part of my journey." Steve had finally met friends he enjoyed being with, and now he had to leave them.

"We did, but truthfully, the diamond sword isn't that important to us," said Henry.

"Do you guys agree with him? The diamond sword is the most powerful sword. Do you have one?" Steve asked as he looked at Max and Lucy.

They sat quietly. None of them had a

diamond sword, and they wanted one. They didn't know what to say.

"I'm going on my own," Steve announced. "I'm going to mine for diamonds, and I'm going to make that sword. Then I'll use an enchantment table to make it even more powerful!" Steve began to leave the group where they sat in a field of skeleton corpses and a pile of bones.

"Do you want any bones, Steve?" Lucy called out.

"Steve, come back," Max pleaded. "I'll help you find the diamonds."

"You will?" Steve turned around.

"Yes," Max said. "I've always wanted to have a super powerful awesome diamond sword. I've never had one before. And I've never been to a party before."

"Seriously?" asked Steve.

"Yes. I want that sword," Max said. "I don't care what Henry says. I think he's afraid we aren't going to find the diamonds to make the swords."

"That's not true!" Henry said. He was quite mad.

"Then why are you being so difficult?" Lucy was annoyed.

"I can find the diamonds without you," Henry told the group, "but I just worry that you can't find them on your own, and I'd feel bad."

The group didn't question Henry, because they knew he was upset and had made a mistake.

"Come with us," said Steve.

With his head down, Henry said, "I was wrong. I'm going to help you, too. It isn't often that you run across someone who actually wants to help villagers."

"I want to see your wheat farm, and I want to dance to those CDs," said Lucy.

The group set off to go on the ultimate diamond mining experience. As the sun began to rise, they heard barking coming from the distance.

"Good thing we have these bones," said Max.

9
TAMING THE WOLF

Armed with pickaxes, the gang began to mine for diamonds. They walked down a staircase in the Overworld and headed deep underneath the ground. The walls around them were layered with multicolored blocks. They broke away at each one carefully. The deeper they got, the more hopeful Steve was that they'd find diamonds. He knew they were only found deep within the surface. Sometimes he heard people would have to go farther than sixteen layers down to find diamonds.

"I think I found something," Lucy called out as she broke through a wall with her pickaxe.

Steve rushed over, hoping he'd see a glimmering blue diamond, but it was just gravel.

"You have to watch out for gravel," Max told the group. "It can fall on us. Let's try to create a mineshaft—that will help us."

Henry placed a torch on the wall for light

while they cracked through the walls of their tunnel to create a mineshaft.

"You have to dig really deep to find diamonds," Henry informed the group.

"Finding forty seems impossible," Lucy said glumly.

Steve used all of his strength to break through the walls. With each blow, he was careful that lava wasn't oozing out from the other side of the wall. It would only take seconds to flood the room and kill them all. When they saw a drop of lava, the group evacuated through a hole in the tunnel.

A cold wind swept through the group, and they emerged into a field of white powder.

"What is this?" Steve shivered, blinded by the seemingly never-ending world of white sand.

"It's snow!" beamed Henry. "We're in the arctic."

"I love it," Lucy said as she ran around and playfully started to throw snowballs in the air. "I haven't been in the Arctic biome in a long time. I forgot how much fun it is."

"Let's build a snowman!" suggested Max.

"Can we do that?" Steve asked sheepishly.

"We can do anything we want," replied Max. "We can build an igloo!"

The cold air felt funny in Steve's lungs.

He had never been in the cold before, and he wished he had a wool coat. He didn't want his friends to know how awkward the cold weather made him feel. He wondered why they all seemed to enjoy it.

"Join us!" Lucy said to Steve. "It feels funny at first, but you'll get used to it and have fun!"

Steve felt like she had read his mind. Would he really get used to this cold weather? As he watched his friends having the time of their lives in the snow, he realized Lucy might be right. He had to relax and enjoy this biome.

Steve grabbed a mound of snow and started to help his friends make a snowman when he heard something breathing heavily.

"What's that?" he asked.

The gang didn't seem to hear it and happily continued playing in the snow.

"I'm a snow princess," Lucy said as she danced around Max and Henry, who were hard at work on their snowman.

"Too bad we're not at your wheat farm," Henry said. "We could really use a carrot for the nose."

"I know!" Max agreed. "I wonder what we can use for the eyes!"

But Steve couldn't pay attention to the snowman. He could hear something panting in the distance. It sounded like a group of wild animals, and he was scared.

"I hear something breathing," Steve told the gang, but nobody listened to him.

Max ran up a large hill covered with snow.

"I can see something," Max called out.

"I told you!" Steve called out to Max.

"It's a frozen river. I bet we could slip around and skate."

"But I hear something breathing!" Steve screamed. "Am I the only one?"

"Ice skating!" Lucy said. "I love ice skating!"

Suddenly a pack of white wolves emerged from behind a snow-covered tree. Their black eyes stood out as their white fur was camouflaged in the snowy landscape.

"I told you I heard something!" Steve shouted out as the pack raced toward the group.

"Get your weapons," Henry told everyone. He took out a sword, and the wolf pack ran away, rushing through the frosted terrain. Their paws left wet imprints in the snow.

"Good job, Henry!" Lucy said with a smile and a handful of snow. "You scared them!"

Yet one lone wolf remained, and it approached Steve. Its menacing, sharp teeth shined in the snowy landscape.

"I have a bone," Steve announced as Henry, Lucy, and Max held snowballs at the ready to battle the growling, hostile wolf.

Slowly the wolf joined Steve and inspected the bone carefully. The wolf's nose brushed up against the skeleton bone. Steve gave him the bone, and the wolf began to roll happily on the ground. A red collar appeared around its neck.

"It's tame!" exclaimed Max.

"You have a pet," Lucy said as she walked over and touched the tame wolf, which was now the same as a dog.

"Let's make an anvil and use our name tag," Henry suggested as he and Max joined Lucy to play with the dog.

The wolf shook the snow from its fur and looked up at Steve. It was Steve's pet, and he had complete control over it. For the rest of Steve's time in the Minecraft world, this wolf would be loyal to him. Wolves had the ability to teleport themselves when they needed to be by their owners to protect them. They were loyal for life.

Steve used the anvil and named the dog Rufus. "I'm going to call you Rufus," he told the wolf. "I have a pet ocelot named Snuggles that I have been watching for a long time. You two better get along well."

The wolf gave Steve a nose bump as the group continued working on their snowman and igloo. Steve relaxed and played with his new pet. He tried to teach it how to sit and planned adventures with the pet wolf.

"It likes you!" Lucy said with a smile.

Rufus ran over to the snowman that Max and Henry finished.

"Isn't the snow fun?" Lucy asked Steve.

"Yes," he agreed.

"Don't you wish we could stay here for a while?" Max said as he stood by the snowman.

"But we have diamonds to search for and villagers to save," Steve told the group to gently remind them of their real plans.

They agreed. This was a fun break, but they had a mission they had promised to finish.

Rufus followed closely behind Steve as the group shoveled their way deep beneath the icy surface in search of an abandoned mineshaft that might be filled with diamonds.

Steve took one last look at the wintery world. It seemed magical, as snow slowly dropped from the sky. He brushed the watery snow from his eyes.

"Isn't it beautiful?" Lucy asked him as their pickaxes took them farther from the surface and closer to Steve's dream.

The mines beneath the snow-covered ground were empty. Steve was beginning to lose hope, but his wolf Rufus was just happy to be on an adventure.

"We'll find diamonds," Lucy said, trying to cheer him up while they made their way to the surface.

They broke through the ceiling above them, and the sun shined. The humid air felt sticky on Steve's skin.

Steve stepped out and into a marshy pit. "Ugh," he said as he shook the water from his boots.

"It's the swamp," said Max, looking out at the water coated with lily pads. Rufus walked over to the lily pads and began to drink from the water.

The water was a deep blue, and the sky had a purplish glow. Night was beginning to fall, and the full moon was growing brighter by the minute. Steve had never seen anything so vibrant yet spooky. In the swamp, sugar canes and vine-covered trees sprouted from patches of water.

"Look at that yucky green water," Steve said as he pointed to a patch of what seemed to be polluted water.

"That's not water!" shouted Max. "That's slime!"

The green blocks of slime inched toward the group. Henry took out his bow and arrow. He fired a shot at the slime. An enormous slimeball oozed through the evening sky and shot slime in every direction. The group shielded themselves from the green gooey substance.

Henry grabbed vines and said, "We can create a ladder to escape the slimes."

Max piled blocks behind them to break their fall while the gang climbed high above the swamp.

"The moon is getting bigger," said Lucy

"Or we're just getting closer," added Max

"No, it's a full moon," said Henry, whose voice seemed to shake as he spit out the last few words, "and that means one thing—witches!"

"Witches?" Steve had enough. They were still hiding from the slime, and now they had to be on the lookout for witches.

"I'm going to—" Henry cried out as he fell

from the ladder of vines. The blocks broke his fall, but he couldn't get back on the vines and landed on the ground below.

"We have to help him," Steve said while he climbed down and found himself surrounded by three slimes.

Lucy adjusted her bow and arrow as she made her way down the vines. She shot one slime. Steve backed away, avoiding being drenched with a slimeball. Suddenly a mini-slime jumped on Steve and made him lose energy. He hit the slime and it bounced off his skin.

Max jumped from the ladder and plunged his sword into the slimes. Green guts flew through the air.

Steve ran over to Henry, "Are you okay?"

"Yes, but look behind you!" warned Henry. "It's a witch hut."

The brown building stood on the grassy marshland. Above it, the moon grew larger, filling the sky as the stars glistened. A small woman opened the front door. She was drinking a tiny glass filled with a potion.

"A witch!" Lucy said as she ran. "Watch out Steve, she's drinking a speed potion. We have to move fast."

Steve grabbed Henry by the arm and pulled him from the swampy ground and away from the witch. Rufus followed Steve while barking at the witches, but wolves had no effect on this evil mob.

The witch looked ahead as she swiftly moved through the swamp right behind the treasure hunters. Her lavender eyes darkened as her lips swallowed more foul liquids. The witch hat flopped, and her purple and green robe blew in the wind as she charged toward them.

When Steve looked back to see her evil face, with its large nose and wart, a purple glow emanated from her body. The witch tossed a potion at the group and immediately they began to slow.

"She got us!" screamed Henry.

"It's a potion of weakness," added Max.

The witch began to change color. The purple mist surrounding her grew darker as she drank more potions.

"She's going to splash more potions at us," warned Lucy. "I have some potions that can help us." Lucy grabbed a potion of strength from her inventory. "This should work."

Max ran toward the witch, lunging at her with his sword. She splashed another potion at Max, and a drop of the potion touched his skin.

"It's poison," Max said as he started to feel weak and sick. His food bar started to turn green.

"What can we do for Max?" asked Steve.

"The poison doesn't last that long," said Lucy, "but he needs to go somewhere and rest. We need to get out of here so Max can recover."

Meanwhile Henry was battling the witch. The witch jumped, missing the blow from Henry's sword. Max was the master at battle, and Henry couldn't fill his shoes. Steve joined Henry and struck the witch, but she didn't get hurt. She pulled out another bottle and started to drink a new potion. This potion gave her even more strength than before, making her even harder to fight. The witch took out another splash potion and aimed it at Steve and Henry.

Henry grabbed Steve and they began to climb the vines. Lucy rushed toward the witch and knocked her out with a well-placed arrow.

"Good job, Lucy!" exclaimed Henry.

The two friends climbed down from the vines and stood by Max. "Where can we take him?" asked Henry.

Steve grabbed a bottle of weakness potion that had fallen on the ground. He put it in his inventory to help cure Eliot the blacksmith.

Steve stared at the dark blue water in the distance. "We need to build boats," suggested Steve.

The group quickly gathered wooden planks from their inventory and started crafting four small boats.

"Do you have enough energy to go in a boat?" asked Lucy.

Max nodded his head. He might have been weak, but sailing away from this witch-infested swamp was his only chance for survival.

"Keep an eye out for witches," Henry told Max as the gang worked on the boats.

Max could see another witch running through the swampland. He told them, "There's one running our way. She must have a swift potion. She's moving fast."

Lucy charged at the witch, but the witch threw out a splash potion of slowness and Lucy's pace began to decrease. A skeleton emerged from the shadows.

"Skeletons and witches. It's just like Halloween," Henry called out as he raced to save Lucy. He took out his bow and fired an arrow at the witch. It knocked her to the ground and defeated her. A glass bottle fell from the witch's hands, and Henry reached to pick it up.

"Trick or treat," he said with a smile as he lunged toward the skeleton, who fell back with a loud clang. Henry grabbed a bone from the skeleton.

"Looks like we have a lot of treats!" he exclaimed as he showed the group.

"Let's get on the boats," Lucy said while she walked slowly toward the boats. She watched for any other hostile mobs that might be lurking in this spooky swamp-filled land, which was only lit by a full moon.

They placed the boats in the water. The four little boats sailed away from the swamp waters and into the calm sea.

"We can use the stars to guide us," Max said as he looked up and pointed out the North Star and Orion.

"It's so peaceful out here," Steve said as he sat in the boat with Rufus swimming next to him. He felt safe from mobs and was enjoying the ride. Although his wheat farm was near the ocean, this was his first boat ride.

"Maybe you should be a sailor," Henry joked from his boat.

The four boats floated right next to one another. Steve stood up, and his boat rocked a bit. He said, "I wonder how long it will take us before we see land."

It seemed like the ocean went on forever. Suddenly, Steve's boat hit something. *Thump!*

"What was that?" Steve asked as he looked out to inspect the damage.

Max's boat fell hard against the same object,

and he added, "I think our boats are crashing!"

"It's squid!" Henry said and pointed to the blue squid with tentacles that reached toward the boat.

"My boat is sinking!" screamed Steve.

Before Lucy or Henry could offer room on their boats, two more loud thumps were heard.

"We've all been hit!" yelled Henry.

"What are we going to do?" asked Steve nervously.

"What do you think we're going to do?" Henry said as he jumped overboard. "We're going to swim!"

The gang dove from their boats into the sea. Rufus swam next to Steve as they searched for land in this aquatic world. It felt like they were swimming forever. Max was exhausted. The witch's potion had seriously decreased his strength. When they thought they couldn't swim another stroke, they saw land.

"An island!" Max screamed for joy.

They swam to shore and found themselves on an abandoned island. Lucy spotted a chicken and took out her bow and arrow.

"We need to eat," Lucy told the group as she offered them each some chicken.

The sun was rising, and Steve walked around the small island to see if there were any resources.

"Look at those eggs," Steve said as he kneeled down to get a closer look.

"Those are silverfish eggs. They can kill you," Henry informed Steve.

Steve immediately took out his sword and began to destroy them before Max had the chance to spit out the word "Stop!"

The eggs broke open and the silverfish were born.

"A griefer put them here. They leave them, because people who don't know about the eggs try to destroy them to kill the silverfish. They don't know that's how silverfish are spawned," Henry told Steve.

"Build a pillar," Max yelled at Steve.

Steve quickly constructed a two-block pillar for the group. Lucy grabbed a handful of gravel and threw it on the silverfish, which destroyed them.

"I don't trust this island. I feel like its booby trapped by a griefer," Henry said as he jumped down from the pillar.

"I bet that's because there's something valuable here, and they want to stop us from getting it," said Lucy.

Max looked out, saw a cave, and said, "I bet that's what they want to keep us from."

"The cave?" asked Steve as Rufus stood next to him.

"I'm pretty sure that's where we're going to find our diamonds," Henry said and walked toward the cave. The group followed him. Steve grabbed a pickaxe from his inventory.

"Let's go diamond hunting!" Steve said with a wide grin.

11
DIAMONDS AND LAVA

With pickaxes in hand, they mined deeper and deeper into the ground.

As Steve looked at his shiny pickaxe, he thought about the tools he had gotten from Eliot, and one of the last conversations they had before the zombie attack. Eliot had been working in the blacksmith shop, and Steve was trading emeralds for the iron pickaxe.

"One day, I'm going to have a diamond pickaxe," said Steve.

"You'll have to go out and find that on your own. My shop doesn't have anything that valuable," replied Eliot.

If only Eliot knew Steve was finally mining for diamonds and trying to craft a diamond sword. He'd never believe scaredy-cat Steve was actually on an adventure. Of course, Steve didn't even know if he'd ever see Eliot again and, if he did, if he could save him from the life of a zombie.

"Look what I found," Max called out.

It was an abandoned mineshaft. The group made a tunnel and entered the mineshaft.

"This is a good sign," Lucy told the group. "I've found diamonds in a mineshaft."

Within seconds, blue dots glistened on the walls.

"Diamonds!" Steve screamed with joy.

As they picked the first diamonds from the mine's surface, a wall of bedrock instantly appeared in front of them and trapped the group.

"A griefer!" screamed Henry.

"The griefer has trapped us!" Lucy began to cry. "Why would they do that?"

"They want the diamonds, too! I told you those silverfish eggs were a trap. I bet they never thought we'd get this far," Henry said.

"The griefer must have seen us coming and put the eggs there," added Max.

"But we need those diamonds. We have to save the villagers!" Steve exclaimed. He was frustrated. They had come so far, and now a griefer was going to steal their diamonds and trap them.

Max began to break away at a stone wall with his pickaxe. He said, "We have to get out of here. We can't let him get the diamonds."

The group furiously knocked the wall down,

but there was another wall behind it.

"This could take forever!" Lucy was exhausted.

"I'm sure this is the last wall. The mine isn't that big," said Henry.

"By the time we reach the other side, the diamonds will be gone and so will the griefer," Steve said, still upset.

When the last bits of the wall crumbled to the ground, they were face-to-face with the griefer.

"You tried to attack us with silverfish!" Max called out to the griefer, who was wearing an orange helmet and holding four diamonds in his hands.

"These are my diamonds," the griefer said as he took a diamond sword out and held it close to the group.

"You trapped us!" Lucy said as she held her sword tightly. She was ready to fight.

"Lucy, don't," said Henry. "He's not worth the fight. I don't want to see you get hurt battling a tricky thief."

"These are my diamonds!" the griefer repeated.

The group was worried that he was with other griefers and they'd be outnumbered, but these cunning evil griefers usually traveled alone.

"Maybe we can share the diamonds," suggested Steve.

"Share?" the griefer said as he began to laugh. "I don't share."

"Then we'll have to battle," Henry said, and he walked close to the griefer with his sword in hand.

Steve could see a spider's red eyes staring at him. The spider quietly crawled behind the griefer. Steve pushed the griefer against the wall. The griefer's head banged against the spider, which began to attack the griefer. The griefer fell to the ground, and Max destroyed the spider with his sword.

"The spider saved the day!" exclaimed Lucy as she ran to the wall and started to collect as many diamonds as she could fit in her inventory.

"I hate griefers," Max said, "but I love diamonds."

"I bet there are even more than forty!" Steve said as he picked the blue jewels from the wall of the abandoned mineshaft.

"Don't get carried away," Henry said while he started to count the diamonds.

The walls of the mine were lined with blue blocks, and the gang mined as fast as they could.

"We need to be careful," warned Henry. "I

think I hear lava flowing behind this wall."

The group filled their inventories with diamonds as they slowly extracted the blocks from the wall without unleashing a waterfall of lava.

"The villagers are going to be saved!" said Steve happily.

"How are we going to get back to the village?" asked Lucy.

"I have a portal in the Nether that can bring us to the village," Steve said. He picked away as he told the group his plan for making their way back to the village.

"I've never been to the Nether!" Lucy said, then she added that she had heard stories about the Nether and knew it could be a deathtrap.

"I bet you guys didn't think we'd ever have an inventory overflowing with diamonds," Steve said proudly.

"Together we can do anything!" Henry said while he looked through his inventory. He seemed satisfied with their conquest. Henry sat on the floor with Steve as they counted the diamonds.

"Don't get too relaxed," warned Max. "It's not time to count the loot. We're still deep underground in a mine. Anything can happen."

"We have forty! Just like we planned!"

exclaimed Steve.

Lucy picked the last diamond from the wall and said, "Max is right, we have to get out of here." She pointed to a large spider that crawled up the wall of the cave and leapt at the group.

With a single swing of Max's gold sword, the spider fell on its back. He said, "Once we craft the diamond swords, we'll be even more powerful."

"Swords?" questioned Steve. "I thought we were just making one sword out of diamonds, and I would use it to destroy the zombies."

"One sword?" Henry asked, shocked. "Now you're acting like a griefer and are just thinking about yourself."

Steve pondered Henry's comment. He wondered if it would be better if they all had swords and were able to fight as a team, rather than him battling the zombies with one super awesome powerful sword. He used his crafting table to make pickaxes for the group. He gave them out to his friends.

"You'll let us have diamond pickaxes, but you won't make us swords?" Lucy asked, perplexed.

"If we all have diamond pickaxes, we can get out of here faster," Steve announced.

"Are you just trying to save yourself?" Max asked. He was very annoyed.

"We don't even have an enchantment table," Henry told everyone. "So these diamonds are useless when making a super awesome powerful sword."

Lucy held the pickaxe. "This looks super powerful. But you're right—to have a super powerful sword, you need an enchantment table."

Steve knew the group was right. He also didn't know what had come over him. Why had he become greedy? The group should all have swords, especially if they were going to help him save his village.

"We can talk about this later," Lucy said as she started to bang through the wall to mine her way out of the tunnel. "We need to get out of here."

"I don't want to go with Steve if he's going to be greedy," said Max.

Henry agreed, "Take your diamonds, Steve. You're on your own."

Steve looked at his friends. He changed his plan and said, "Let's make four swords out of ten diamonds each. I have no idea what got in to me. I was acting like Henry."

Henry shot Steve a dirty look and retorted, "Seriously, dude, this is no time to pick fights. We need to stick together."

"You're right. I guess I wanted to be the hero

on my own and save my villagers," said Steve.

"They're not your villagers," Lucy remarked.

"Steve, watch out!" Henry grabbed Steve's hand as they ran through the tunnel. Hot orange lava began to rush through a hole in the wall.

12
IT'S NETHER ENDING

The air was a sea of purple mist as steve used the last of his obsidian to construct a portal to the Nether, and they all ran through, narrowly escaping the accidental lava flow on the other side.

"Look, a lava waterfall," Lucy said as she pointed to the waterfall that flowed in front of their portal. "There's something really pretty about the Nether, but it also seems extremely deadly."

Steve would never consider himself an expert at anything, especially traveling with his new treasure hunting friends, but he had experience in the Nether and knew many survival skills.

"It looks scarier than it is," Steve told the group. He led them over a bridge and toward the portal that would take them back to the Overworld and his village.

"It's so hot here, and so red," Lucy said. She looked out from the bridge to the maroon expanse of this foreign land.

As they made their way off the bridge, Lucy ran toward a patch of red flowers.

"I didn't know flowers grew in the Nether," said Max.

"They're beautiful," she said as she smelled them.

"Look out!" Henry took out his bow and arrow and shot a blaze that flew high above him. Fire flew down at them, landing on the flowers.

"You saved us!" said Steve.

"But you killed the flowers," Lucy said, upset.

"*Shhh*!" Steve held his finger to his lips. "Do you hear that?"

"What?" asked Henry.

"I hear someone talking," Steve whispered.

"I don't hear anything," Lucy said as she listened.

"We have to make sure nobody steals these diamonds," Steve said warily. What if somebody saw them get the diamonds and followed them? Or what if the griefer from earlier wasn't working alone?

"Now I hear," said Lucy as she looked around to see if she could find the people who were talking.

"Over there," Max said and pointed to two

people standing by a pool of lava.

"Hide the diamonds," Steve told the group as the two strangers approached them.

They looked very odd. Their skin was the color of rainbows. They walked over to the gang. One of them had a compass in his hand.

"We're lost. Can you help us?" the one with the compass asked them.

"Compasses don't work in the Nether," Steve replied, convinced these were two tricksters who were about to attack them.

Steve remembered the Nether fortress that had been looted. Maybe these were the people who took the jewels from there.

"Where are you from?" Steve asked.

"We are from the Overworld. We used a portal and wound up here," replied one of the rainbow men.

Rufus barked at the rainbow men, and Steve took that as a sign they might be bad. The wolf kept barking, and Steve put his hand on his sword.

"Look out," shouted the other rainbow man. Behind the rainbow men marched two gigantic gray skeletons.

"Wither skeletons!" Henry cried out.

Rufus wasn't barking at the rainbow men, but at the evil wither skeletons. The gray beasts lashed at the group and one hit Steve with its stone sword. He held tightly to the diamonds as he dropped to the ground.

Max took out his gold sword and hit one of the skeletons. *Crunch!* The skeleton's bones lay on the ground.

A rainbow man and the remaining wither skeleton began to fight. Their swords danced through the air as the fight intensified.

The rainbow man knocked the wither skeleton's sword from his hand and went in for the final blow, destroying the skeleton.

"We did it!" Steve said as he lifted himself from the ground.

"No, I did it," said the rainbow man, who turned to Steve and struck him with his sword. Steve cried out in pain.

"Now give us the diamonds," demanded the other rainbow man.

"We don't have any diamonds," Lucy said, her voice quivering.

"You're lying. We followed you from the mineshaft," one of the rainbow men retorted. He moved closer to Lucy, and his sword came very close to her face.

Two blazes flew through the night sky. They spotted the group below and their mouths opened while fireballs shot out. Lucy jumped, the fireball missing her and striking one of the rainbow men. The other rainbow guy ran toward his friend and was engulfed in flames.

"So long griefers," Lucy called out as the group ran through the red-hot Nether in search of Steve's portal.

It seemed like hours of searching when Henry pointed to a fortress. "Is that the fortress that you visited?" he asked.

Steve didn't know. Everything looked the same, and he was tired, confused, and hungry.

"I'm not sure," he replied as they walked toward the fortress.

"Don't worry," Lucy said with a smile. "We need to get these diamonds crafted into swords before we can head back anyway. And first we have to—"

Max interrupted, "Make obsidian!"

"Yes," said Henry, "and we all know the best way to do that is with lava."

They stopped. A sea of lava was before them. Lucy tripped.

"Don't fall in!" Max screamed.

13

JOURNEY TO THE END

Henry grabbed lucy to make sure she didn't fall into the hot lava. To make obsidian, they needed lava and water, but the process was extremely dangerous. After Lucy nearly fell into the pool, the group was worried they'd never be able to make the obsidian, which was needed to create an enchantment table.

"If we don't have an enchantment table to make powerful swords, these diamonds are useless," said Steve with a frown. Rufus wagged his tail as he stood by his master, clearly not understanding the grimness of the situation.

"I'm going to try again," Lucy said. She bravely put her bucket by the lava but quickly pushed her hand back and said, "I'm going to get burned. This isn't going to work."

"We can't do this," Max announced to the group.

"I have a plan," Henry said with a smile. "You're not going to be happy about it, but I think we should go to The End."

"The End?" Lucy asked and let out a gasp.

"That's where the Ender Dragon lives," Steve's voice shook.

He had only read about the Ender Dragon. The Ender Dragon was the head of the Endermen, and surviving an attack from this beast seemed impossible.

"The Ender Dragon could kill us all in seconds," Max told Henry.

"In The End, there are pillars of obsidian. We can make an enchantment table and get a portal to the Overworld," Henry replied.

"It's not worth it," Steve protested. "We can make obsidian here."

Steve grabbed the bucket and tried to get lava, but he couldn't extract the lava without falling in. It was too tricky. Rufus looked at the lava and walked away.

"How do we get to The End?" Steve asked as he sat by the pool of lava.

"We need to make a portal," Henry told the group. "It can only be created in a Nether fortress."

The fortress was off in the distance. There was dead silence among the friends until Steve said, "I'm nervous. I've never been to The End."

"Me either," said Lucy, "but we need to get that obsidian. How else are we going to help your villagers?"

"I've never been there either," said Max.

Henry spit out, "This will be my first time, too."

"What?!" Steve was shocked. "You're leading us to a place you know nothing about. We could all get killed."

"I believe as a group we have the power to beat the Ender Dragon," Henry said to defend his plan.

"You really believe in us," Steve said. He was surprised.

"Yes, look at how far we've come. We have forty diamonds!" said Henry proudly.

Luckily, the Nether fortress wasn't guarded by a blaze, and they made their way to the entrance. Inside the red fortress, they searched for blaze spawn.

"We need to destroy the blaze spawn and get the blaze rods to make our portal to The End," said Henry.

A couple of Endermen walked through the fortress. Steve grabbed his sword and lunged at the Endermen. One fell onto the blocks of the Nether fortress.

"I didn't think Endermen were in the Nether," Lucy said as she pointed to the Enderman who lurked through the fortress.

"They must have followed us through the

portal," said Max.

"Help," Steve yelled to his friends. "Grab the Ender pearls."

When an Enderman was destroyed, he dropped Ender pearls. The gang needed these to make the Eye of Ender, which was essential in the creation of a portal to The End.

Max joined Henry as they let fly arrow after arrow from their bows until the Endermen were gone and they had enough Ender pearls to get to The End.

"It's funny," Steve remarked. "When I was here alone, I kept getting attacked by blazes, and now we can't even find blaze spawn."

"And we need to find it fast, because I'm losing energy. My food bar is quite low," Lucy said as she picked up the last of the Ender pearls.

It was true, the group was running low on energy. It had been a while since Lucy had slayed the chicken for the group. They needed to make their way to The End quickly.

"I think I see a blaze spawn," Max said as he pointed to a room. The group went to investigate, but it was empty.

Suddenly, two shot across the room. "Get them!" shouted Henry.

The blazes unleashed a shower of fire, and the group jumped back, almost falling into a waterfall of lava that flowed through the center of the fortress.

Max used his bow and arrow to knock one blaze to the ground as the other three friends grabbed the blaze rods.

Three more blazes flew by and started firing. Steve reluctantly suggested using the Enchanted Golden Apple he was saving for Eliot the blacksmith. Now that he had the weakness potion from the witches, he needed that Golden Apple for Eliot. He thought of Eliot spending the rest of his life as a zombie. Rufus's barking stopped his mind from wandering, and he was ready to attack.

"I have a few we can use," Lucy said, and the group was shielded from the blaze's mighty blows. With swords and bows, the team beat the blazes.

"We have enough blaze rods," Steve said. He was excited as he picked up the last rods.

Henry started to build the portal to The End while the others watched for hostile mobs, such as slimy magma cubes.

They built the Ender Portal in a large room in the fortress. The rectangular portal had twelve Eyes of Ender surrounding it. Black dust flew above the top of the portal.

"I don't want to go in!" shouted Steve.

"We have to do it fast," demanded Henry.

"I thought that once you go to The End, you never come back!" Steve was shaking.

"No, we can go back to the Overworld once we defeat the Ender Dragon," Lucy said. She acted like defeating the Ender Dragon was some easy task. It was a death trap—an impossibility—but before Steve had a chance to run away, Henry pushed him through the portal. The others followed, and they drifted down to The End.

14
THE ENDER DRAGON

The end was dark with floating green platforms. The group landed on a platform, staring at a large obsidian pillar.

"Look," Henry pointed out. "The pillars are made of obsidian. We just need to get some blocks and defeat the dragon, and we can go."

"Do you see the crystals on top of the pillars?" Steve asked Henry.

"Yes," he replied.

"Do you know what that's for?" asked Steve, though he already knew the answer. Everyone did. Those crystals helped the Ender Dragon get energy. Even if you struck the Ender Dragon, it had many ways to survive. Eating from the crystals was just one of them.

"It doesn't matter," said Henry quite confidently. "We're going to defeat it anyway."

Lucy's legs shook as she walked toward the edge of the platform. "If we fall," she said, pointing to the darkness beneath them, "we will be lost in the void."

"Stay back Rufus," Steve told the wolf. Rufus stood faithfully by his side.

"There's a green surface we can walk on," Steve said as he looked down. "We should build a bridge to that staircase."

The enormous green staircase was a few feet from the platform. The group began to construct a bridge while putting blocks of obsidian in their inventory.

"We have enough obsidian to make an enchantment table," Steve announced.

"But we have to defeat that first," Lucy said. Her hand shook as she pointed to the large black dragon flying toward the group.

The dragon's purple eyes shined through the dark skies that filled The End. Below the dragon was an army of Endermen.

Max shot arrows at the dragon. One struck the beast in the head, and it dropped from the sky toward the group of Endermen below, coming close to the Endermen.

"We did it!" Steve cried out joyfully.

"It's not that easy," Max said as he shot another arrow. The dragon got up and flew toward the group. It was ready to attack.

"We've definitely annoyed it," said Max as he shot another arrow, but it missed.

Henry, Lucy, and Steve also shot at the beast. "At least there are four of us and only one of him," Lucy said, striking the flying beast with her arrow.

The dragon made a deafening roar as the arrow pierced its scaly skin. The group wanted to cover their ears, but they couldn't let go of their weapons.

"The dragon's health isn't good. We have a chance," announced Henry.

The dragon slowly made its way to the crystals and started to eat. It seemed unaffected by Steve's arrow, which struck its underbelly.

"We need to destroy the crystals," Lucy told the group. "If we can do that, the dragon has no way to get energy."

The group shot at the crystals and destroyed them, but the dragon had already eaten enough, and it flew at them with great speed.

They ducked as the growling dragon flew above them. Max struck the dragon with an arrow. Rufus barked, but the Ender Dragon didn't pay attention to the wolf.

The dragon's next roar was louder than the first. The beast was ready to destroy this crew that dared to attempt to defeat it. The powerful dragon didn't want to show weakness, but it was in pain, and the group could see they were winning.

"We must have hurt it. Keep shooting, guys," Henry said as the team tried to strike the flying menace again. This time they hoped it would be the blow that killed the Ender Dragon.

"Endermen!" Steve screamed as Endermen walked across the bridge. Steve grabbed pumpkins from his inventory. "If we put these on our heads, they won't notice us."

Endermen wouldn't notice them if they wore these masks. Wearing pumpkin heads, the group shot at the Ender Dragon. With each hit, the dragon's cries grew louder and angrier. It flew back toward them, ready to wipe them out.

"It's over!" Steve shouted, wanting to cover his eyes.

"Not yet it's not!" Max yelled as his arrow struck the dragon right between the eyes, and it fell to the ground.

"Is it dead?" Lucy asked.

"Does this answer your question?" Henry said as he pointed to a portal that emerged on the green ground below. The portal signified their defeat of the Ender Dragon. They had beaten the fiercest creature in the Minecraft world. They were warriors, and once they helped the villagers, they would be heroes.

"We need to make our way back to the Overworld," Steve said as he looked at the portal.

The stairs were shaky as the group walked

toward the field of green blocks and down the hole, surrounded by pillars of fire. On top lay a lone dragon egg.

"I don't want to be here when that hatches," Steve said. He pointed to the egg. The group nodded in agreement as he led Rufus toward the portal.

This time, they were fearless as they entered the portal that would take them back home.

15

GOING HOME

Rufus barked as the group emerged from the portal into a world of green bricks.

"The wheat farm!" Steve exclaimed. He had never been so happy in his life. He could hear Snuggles meowing by the gate.

It was daylight, and the group was safe from zombies. Steve gave the friends a tour of the farm.

Lucy took out her bow and arrow and hit a pig. "Sorry, I was hungry," she said as she offered meat to the gang.

"I have tons of food," Steve said as the friends feasted on carrots and potatoes.

"This place is great!" Max said. The group finally relaxed, enjoying food and Steve's farm.

"We need to make an enchantment table," Steve said. He knew it would be night soon, and they needed to get to the village and battle the zombies to save his friends.

With obsidian, the group enchanted their diamond swords. They were going to battle the zombies, and they had to be prepared.

"Remember, we have to save a diamond so we can make a jukebox," Lucy reminded them. "I want to have a party with the villagers once we save them."

"Yes," Steve replied. He was so focused on saving the villagers that he had forgotten about the CDs they collected during the battle with the skeletons and creepers.

Suddenly, Steve heard barking. Rufus and Snuggles had met each other, and he thought they weren't happy about it. He was wrong—when he walked outside, he saw them playing with each other as the gang finished their diamond creations.

"Look at these swords!" Max said, impressed.

Henry picked up his new diamond sword. Slowly he approached Steve while holding his sword.

"Henry?" asked Steve nervously. "What are you doing?"

"I want all the diamonds," Henry replied. He put the sword close to Steve's face.

"No," Steve said. He took out his sword and was ready to fight. Steve was right all along; he shouldn't have trusted Henry.

"Give us all of your diamonds and carrots, and we'll be on our way," Henry said. Henry swung his sword, and Steve retreated.

Lucy and Max stood by. They didn't know whom to defend.

"Are you guys going to help me?" Steve asked as Henry began to strike Steve but missed.

They said nothing.

"Are you going to help me?" Henry asked them.

Again, silence.

The two fought. Each blocked the other's moves. "Why are you doing this?" Steve asked Henry. "I thought we were friends. Are you a griefer?"

"I'm a treasure hunter, and you have a lot of treasures," Henry screamed.

"This is a griefer move," Steve yelled. "You're attacking me, not stealing treasure. I knew I should have never trusted you, and after all we went through together."

"I knew if I came all this way, I'd be rewarded. Look at your wheat farm. It's filled with so many goodies. I can live off this land for a million lives," said Henry.

Then Lucy screamed. She screamed so loudly that glass shattered in Steve's home.

"Stop!"

Her voice was loud and piercing. Rufus and Snuggles came into the house and stared at her, and Henry dropped his sword.

"You're right, Steve," Lucy said. "We weren't

only treasure hunters. We were griefers, too."

"Were?" asked Henry. "You mean are?"

"No." Lucy looked at Henry and said, "Remember how it felt when that griefer tried to steal our diamonds?"

"Yes." Henry looked at the ground.

"We can't do this to Steve. Yes, we started out wanting to steal his goods, but he's our friend. Think about how much he's done for us. How much we've done for each other."

"But—" Henry tried to speak.

Max interrupted, "We need to stick together and fight the zombies with Steve. This isn't right, Henry. Just because we used to be bad doesn't mean we can't change."

"Yes," Lucy agreed. She was happy to hear Max agree with her. "Max gets it. We have to help Steve. Now give me that diamond sword, Henry. You don't deserve it."

Steve wondered if this was all a trick. Maybe Max and Lucy were just trying to get on his good side, and then they were going to attack him once the zombies were gone. He didn't know what to think. But he looked over at Lucy, and she smiled at him. He realized that he had to trust her, and he had to give Henry another chance.

"Don't take the sword from Henry," Steve told Lucy.

Henry was shocked and asked, "What?"

"Keep it," Steve said. "You're going to help me battle the zombies."

"Seriously, dude?" Henry couldn't believe Steve.

"Look, I know it's your instinct to destroy and steal from people, but I believe you can become a better person. I saw you help us so much when we were searching for the diamonds. I can't believe you were doing that all to steal from me. I mean, that just doesn't make sense. You worked too hard and cared too much."

Henry looked at Steve as Lucy handed the sword back.

"Thank you," Henry said. "I think you're right. I just saw all the diamonds, and I wanted to take them all."

Dusk was approaching. "We need to save the villagers," Steve said as he looked out the window. "Henry, are you going to suit up and join the battle, or are you on your own?"

"I'm one of you guys," Henry said with a smile. They couldn't fight each other, they had to fight zombies.

16

ZOMBIE SHOWDOWN

The sun began to set as the group suited up in armor, packed their diamond swords, and left for the village. Rufus ran behind them, eyeing the landscape for creepers and Endermen. Steve felt his heart beating fast. Despite all of his adventures, he was nervous to see what had happened to the village. Maybe it was too late to save Eliot the blacksmith. Was Avery the librarian still hiding in the library, or was she a zombie, too? And would the Enchanted Golden Apples save them? All of these thoughts were swirling in Steve's head as he approached the once-peaceful village.

The village was empty. The Iron Golem still lay torn apart on the street. Steve and his friends walked through the village looking for any signs of life. He led them to Eliot's blacksmith shop, but it was empty. Where were the villagers hiding? Steve looked under the counter and in the corner of the shop, but he couldn't find anyone. Rufus began to bark and run. A creeper approached but left when it saw the wolf.

"I hear something," Steve said as he walked toward the library.

The group followed Steve into the library. The shelves were broken and books were ripped apart. Many of the books Steve loved to read were on the floor of the library. He went to pick up his favorite book on farming when he saw Avery the librarian hiding behind a shelf.

"Avery!" Steve exclaimed. He was excited to see her. "Are you okay?"

"It's night," she said in a scared whisper. "This is when they come back."

"Where is everyone?" he asked.

"They're hiding at farmer John's house." She stood up.

"Where are the zombies?" Steve asked.

"They'll be back. The one with the armor is impossible. He has a helmet, so he can attack during the day, too. The village has been hiding since you left." She looked at Steve, and he could see the hope in her eyes. She wanted him to save the village, and Steve knew this was his moment. He also knew he couldn't do it without his friends.

"These are my friends," he said, and he introduced Avery to Henry, Lucy, and Max.

"They are going to help me save this village and defeat these evil zombies."

"Thank you," she said, and Henry almost let out a tear as he realized the joy of helping others.

Suddenly, a green-eyed zombie appeared from behind a bookshelf. "Oh no!" Avery cried out.

Henry jumped toward the zombie and destroyed it with a single blow from his newly minted diamond sword.

"See, it is super awesome and powerful!" Henry said and smiled. He hoped the diamond sword would make the zombie battle quick and easy.

Outside the library, the streets filled with zombies. Steve couldn't believe the amount of zombies that walked toward them.

"Maybe this won't be as easy as I thought," Henry said. He stared at his diamond sword.

"If we work together, we have a chance at winning," said Lucy.

"This is my biggest challenge ever, and I'm ready for it," said Max. He ran toward the zombies and knocked out a bunch with the powerful sword.

Steve knew he would have never been able to defeat these zombies alone, and the only chance he had was with the help of his new friends. Steve's emotions overwhelmed him. He looked out at the zombies and realized many were zombie villagers. He recognized a bunch of them, but one face stuck out from the crowd. It was Eliot the blacksmith!

"Eliot!" Steve called out, but Eliot didn't even blink. He had no idea who Steve was. To Eliot, Steve was an enemy and needed to be defeated. Eliot leapt toward Steve. He had to give Eliot the Enchanted Golden Apple, but he also had to defeat the zombies that made their way into the library.

"Hide, Avery!" Steve yelled as the gang fearlessly ran toward the zombies and struck them with their diamond swords.

Eliot the blacksmith walked toward Steve with green eyes that showed that Eliot was ready to attack his friend.

"Eliot! It's me!" Steve pleaded with his friend, but it was useless.

Henry ran toward to Eliot and was ready to attack him. "Stop!" Steve screamed. "He's my friend. Get an Enchanted Golden Apple and a potion of weakness. We need to bring him back to life!"

"Here!" Henry threw a Golden Apple and a potion, and Steve gave both to Eliot. Within a few minutes, Eliot's eye's lost their green color, and he was a normal villager.

"Thank you!" Eliot said happily. "You guys saved me!"

However, there wasn't time for happy reunions. The town was still crawling with zombies, and the group had a job to do.

"You need to hide, Eliot," Steve demanded. "Go with Avery and hide under the shelves at the library."

Eliot ran into the library to take shelter.

"Got one!" Lucy screamed as she knocked a zombie to the ground.

"It seems like no matter how many we destroy, there are still more zombies. Where are they spawning?" asked an exhausted Max.

Zombies' growling could be heard throughout the village.

"I think they keep calling for back up," Steve said. "We just need to fight them all. If we could survive The End, we can do this!"

Steve's diamond sword was as powerful as he imagined. He was happy that it could destroy so many zombies so quickly.

Henry came up behind Steve, and the duo downed a group of zombies. "See how much better we are as a team?" Steve asked as he looked at Henry.

"You're right," Henry said as he used his sword to destroy two zombies.

As Steve made his way through the town,

it seemed like there were more zombies on the ground than walking through the streets.

Then it appeared in front of the team of four. It stood outside Eliot's blacksmith shop. It was the armored zombie.

"That's it!" Steve said and pointed. The group had to come up with a plan.

"We have diamond swords! We can get it!" Max ran toward the zombie. Max struck the zombie in its leg with the sword. The zombie was destroyed, which left Max with the armor.

"You did it!" Steve shouted gleefully.

"No," said Max, "we did it!"

"It doesn't matter! This means the battle is almost over! We destroyed the most powerful zombie!" Steve yelled. He was thrilled.

"You can take the armor," Max said as he gave it to Steve.

"Thanks!" Steve replied, then he grabbed the armor and put it on.

Henry and Lucy fought off zombies as Rufus searched the streets for creepers.

When the last zombie had been destroyed, Steve walked the streets to make sure it was really emptied of the bloodthirsty, green-eyed beasts. When he had checked the last corner of his favorite village, he declared a victory.

"We need to make a new Iron Golem," Steve said as he used his iron to craft a new Golem for the town.

"What happened to the old Golem?" Henry asked.

"A griefer destroyed it to harvest it for iron," Steve told him.

"Griefers can be really bad," Henry said.

As Henry stood thinking about griefers, Eliot, John, and Avery came racing toward Steve.

"You saved our village!" said John the farmer.

"You're my hero!" Eliot the blacksmith said and smiled.

"You saved the day!" Avery called out.

"Thanks. I'm just happy you guys are safe, and now we can rebuild the village. And don't thank me. Thank my friends. I couldn't have done it without them," Steve replied.

Henry watched as all the villagers began to congratulate the others. He stood hidden behind a tree. He wasn't sure what to do. He had never done anything nice for anyone, and this feeling was strange to him. Steve walked over to Henry.

"See how important it is to help others?" Steve asked. "We could rob the villagers of their wares, but it's much better to help them."

"I feel so strange. I've never felt this way before," Henry admitted.

"That's what it feels like to be good," Steve said. "You should join us and let the villagers thank you. You earned it, my friend."

The two walked to the center of the village, where the mood was festive and the villagers emerged from their homes. They didn't have to hide anymore.

"We're going to throw a party on my wheat farm!" Steve announced to the villagers. "I want everyone to come celebrate the destruction of the evil zombies and talk about the plans to secure the village from further attacks."

"We've already constructed a new Iron Golem," Lucy announced as she placed the pumpkin head on the Golem.

"And we should all rejoice in this victory. It wasn't an easy battle, but it was for a good cause," Henry said, and the crowd cheered. He had never felt so happy in his life. Steve was right, helping others felt great.

The team led everyone to the wheat farm. They were ready to have a party! Rufus barked as the sun rose.

Steve had never had so many people in his home, and he was shocked at how much he loved having friends over. The villagers filled his living room. After days of hiding, they were happy to be free of the zombie attack and were thrilled to be in Steve's living room. Most had never been to a party.

Steve handed out red party hats, and the group put them on. Steve placed a table in the living room and filled it with cookies and other goodies. He offered the villagers and his new friends the treats.

Lucy put one of the CDs in the new diamond jukebox, and the villagers began to move about.

"Look at my emeralds," Eliot said as he pointed to the bricks that were lined with emeralds in Steve's house.

"Those are my emeralds," Steve said and smiled. "I traded them."

"That's right," Eliot replied as he also smiled. "You need to come back to my shop and trade again."

"How's your shop?" Steve asked.

"It's almost back to normal. The village is going to take a while to get back to the way it used to be, but thanks to you, we will be able to have a village again."

"And you're not a zombie," Steve said with a smile. "That was quite a zombie battle today."

"You saved the day!" Avery the librarian came over and told Steve.

"No, my friends and I saved the day," Steve said as he brought Henry, Max, and Lucy over to the center of the living room. The villagers stood around them. "These are my best friends, and together we can tackle anything!"

Steve really believed he and his friends could do anything. He thought about telling the villagers about their battle with the Ender Dragon, but he didn't want to brag. But it was a story *he* still couldn't believe, and he wanted to share it with others.

"We were so glad to help you," Henry told the villagers, "but we don't need any thanks. Just seeing how happy and safe you are in the village makes us all happy."

"I love searching for treasure and battling hostile mobs, but until I met Steve, I never realized how important it is to help others," Lucy added as she stood next to Henry.

"You guys taught me so much. I can't imagine that I taught you anything, except what it's like to be afraid of things," Steve told his friends.

"No, you taught us a lot. And we saw you change. You're not so scared anymore," Lucy told Steve.

"You're right! I'm not," Steve said. He was extremely happy. Normally, he'd be afraid to have so many people in his house, but now he rejoiced.

Max walked over to the diamond jukebox.

"I'm glad we saved a diamond to make this jukebox," Lucy said, joining Max.

"I just want to dance!" Max said, and he made the music louder. The group listened to the CDs.

Henry, Lucy, and Max danced as Steve walked over to Eliot to relax.

"I can't wait to just walk into the village and trade my emeralds and coal," Steve told Eliot.

"But you must have so many stories to tell. You and your friends had so many adventures. How can you stick around here? Don't you want to go exploring?" asked Eliot.

"Yes, Steve," Henry said as he walked over. "Don't you want to treasure hunt with us?"

Avery the librarian joined the group, and Steve pointed to her and said, "I can read about adventures in the books I get from Avery's library."

"I bet the books I have aren't that exciting," said Avery.

"But you got to live it," Eliot the blacksmith told Steve. "That's so incredible."

Steve heard barking and excused himself to check on Rufus. He looked at Rufus, tame and playing with Snuggles. This was where he wanted to be. Yes, treasure hunting was fun and now he wasn't scared, but he liked the idea of being a farmer and building on his wheat farm. While others loved to trek to unfamiliar places, he was excited to sleep in his wool bed. Steve walked back into the party.

"Anybody want carrots?" He asked, offering the goodies to the gang.

"You are so generous," Henry said as he ate the carrots.

"I worked hard and have a lot to share," Steve told him.

The mood at the party was jovial, and the villagers seemed to have no worries. Life was back to normal for Steve.

"Let's play some games," Avery announced, and the gang and the villagers had races through the wheat farm.

"Beat you!" Max exclaimed and smiled as he raced Steve across the green landscape of

Steve's farm.

This was the best—and only—party Steve ever held. But the day was almost over, and like all good parties, it had to come to an end.

18
I HATE GOODBYES

The moon appeared in the sky. the villagers made their way back to their homes since it was getting dark. They had a long day ahead of them tomorrow as they cleaned up their village from the zombie war. As the villagers thanked Steve and left, Steve sat in his home with his friends.

"I used to be afraid to be out of my bed at night," Steve told the group. "And I never had a visitor at my house."

"You could have fooled me. You threw the best party," Henry told him.

Steve stared at the moon. It was so bright; it stood out in the starry skies.

"What are you staring at? Are you afraid the Ender Dragon is coming after you?" Lucy joked.

"I'm looking at the moon," Steve said quite seriously. "I think I want to explore the moon. Are you guys in?"

"Funny, you were afraid to get out of your bed earlier this week, and now you want to travel to the moon?" Max asked. He was happy to see his friend become fearless.

"Well, would you guys want to join me?" Steve repeated his request.

"I think that sounds fun!" said Lucy.

"I have to figure out how we could get there first, then we can explore space. It will take a while though. Do you guys want to stay here and help me work on it?" Steve asked the group. Steve wanted a period of rest when he could just build on his farm and trade with his villager friends. Plus, he didn't want to stay on the moon forever, he just wanted to take a trip and then return to his life on the wheat farm.

"Truthfully, I think we want to go treasure hunting," Henry said. "We aren't good at sticking around one place. We like to see everything. We're not only treasure hunters, we're also thrill seekers."

"We miss searching for treasures," Lucy told Steve. "I mean, we loved helping you, but that's not where our heart is. We love to find new stuff and use everything in our inventory."

"Yeah, we're not hoarders," joked Henry.

"Hey! Hoarders have a lot of useful stuff. If I didn't have milk, you'd still be in a cave sick from a spider bite," Steve said, defending himself.

"I was just joking, but you're right—you are

very prepared," Henry said as he smiled.

"I learned a lot from this adventure. I learned it's important to save, but it's also important to share," said Steve.

"I'm going to miss you, Steve," said Lucy.

"But we have to go, because I haven't blown anything up in days," sighed Henry. "I miss the thrill of finding those four treasure chests and making my escape from the temple with the loot in my hand. That's the best feeling in the world."

"I know what you mean," agreed Max.

"Yes, that's what we love doing. And I want to go back to the snow biome and play. I love exploring!" Lucy said as she looked up at the sky. "But the moon seems like a fantastic place to travel."

Henry sat next to Steve, stared at him, and said, "Steve, you taught me how to be good and why I shouldn't be a griefer. I owe you my life for that."

"I know. I understand," Steve said. He knew his friends had different goals, and he couldn't stop them from doing what they loved. They had helped him save his village, and he would always be grateful for their help.

"I'm so glad we met you," Lucy said. She looked at Steve and smiled.

"I'm going to miss all of you," said Steve.

"Why don't you come with us?" asked Henry.

"I'd love to, but I really want to help the villagers rebuild," Steve replied.

"And work on a way to get to the moon, right?" asked Henry.

"Yes," Steve said.

"If you figure it out, give us a call. We'll go with you," Henry said with a smile while Lucy and Max nodded in agreement.

"I'd love that!" Steve said as he walked the gang to the door. They stood on his front porch and looked at the moon.

"I wonder what it's like up there," pondered Lucy.

"I bet there's all kind of cool treasure," said Henry.

"There's only one way to find out," Steve said. He smirked as he looked at the big moon, imagining all the adventures he could have with his new friends in space.

"Goodbye, Steve," said Henry as the group left the wheat farm.

Rufus and Snuggles came out to say goodbye to the three friends.

"I hate saying goodbye," Steve told the group.

"Don't think of goodbye, just think of the next time we say hello," said Max.

Steve smiled as he watched his friends walk off into the distance in search of treasure. He hoped their new diamond swords would protect them as they explored the world.

AN **UNOFFICIAL** GAMER'S NOVEL

THE MYSTERY OF THE GRIEFER'S MARK

WINTER MORGAN